WALPURGIS

THE HAWTHORNE UNIVERSITY WITCH PREQUEL SERIES

BOOK 3

A.L. HAWKE

PHANTOM HEART, LLC

Copyright © 2025 by A.L. Hawke

All rights reserved. No portion of this book may be reproduced, distributed or transmitted in any form or by any electronic or mechanical means, including information storage and retrieval systems, without permission in writing, except by reviewers who may quote brief passages for a review.

ISBN: 978-1-953919-90-8

ISBN: 978-1-953919-97-7 (paperback)

ISBN: 978-1-953919-91-5 (hardcover)

ISBN: 978-1-953919-92-2 (audiobook)

Library of Congress Control Number: 2025919856

This is a work of fiction. It comes directly from the author's imagination. Witchcraft is included to infuse a sense of realism to the novel, but in no way is it supposed to represent actual practicing witchcraft, witches, or the religion of Wicca or Thelema. Any satanic groups portrayed in this series are purely fictional and not intended to represent actual people or organization(s).

The book also includes fictitious names, characters, places, and incidents. Any public names are used solely for creative purposes. Any resemblance to actual people, living or dead, or to companies, institutions, or locales is entirely coincidental or accidental.

Line edited by Stephanie Marshall Ward

Proofread by Alexa B., alexabooks.wixsite.com/authors

Cover Design © 2025 by Brosedesignz

Published by Phantom Heart, LLC

27702 Crown Valley Pkwy, STE D4 #201

Ladera Ranch, CA 92694

Printed and bound in the United States of America

First printing 2025

Learn more about A.L. Hawke at www.alhawke.com

Correspondence: contact@alhawke.com

✽ Formatted with Vellum

1

BURN THE WITCH

WALPURGISNACHT.

Why did Melanie keep saying that? I can't get the image of the demon-freak out of my head—her creepy all-white eyes, her little hands raised high while she grimaces in madness. She kept saying the word for "Walpurgis" in its original German, *Walpurgisnacht*. She said it so much, it felt almost like a tic. At other times she barked it like a dog.

Walpurgisnacht.

Alone in the main hall of Jonathan Brewster Taylor Library, studying at a long wooden table surrounded by the familiar aisles of books, it's always quiet. But this morning it's very quiet. Because everyone's gone home for the summer. There's a stack of books to my right, and a history book opened up discussing the Walpurgis Night. I need to learn everything I can to stop her.

Walpurgis Night is a festival that takes place on the evening of April 30th. It's the day before Hawthorne's better known witch festival: Beltane. Here at Hawthorne, Beltane is a huge ordeal when frat boys drink and dance half-naked, in drunken revelry with bare-breasted ladies near bonfires. Of course, Allie's group loves it. But we really never celebrated Walpurgis. I hadn't even heard of Walpurgis until I looked it up.

The two holidays have a lot in common. Beltane is a Celtic ceremony, whereas Walpurgis is German and Scandinavian. The festival of Walpurgis Night, *Walpurgisnacht* in German, celebrates the life of St. Walpurga, a saint who fought illnesses, like rabies and whooping cough, along with —you guessed it—witch curses. Upon this night, people lit bonfires to burn effigies of witches. And, like so many other Christian holidays—Christmas, Easter—it's likely that this saint's holiday was established by the church on a night already celebrated by pagans. After all, Walpurgis Night and Beltane fall celestially between spring equinox and summer solstice. So witches were probably gathering around bonfires on April 30th way before Saint Walpurga was even born. Under Celtic tradition, Beltane heralds the meeting of the three-headed goddess and the green man. The three-headed goddess represents a woman's youth, middle age, and old age. I suppose the green man with horns represents nature. And, like the Greek god Pan, this depiction fits well with the church's hellish imagery of Satan. Walpurgis is different. In Sweden, on Valborg, they sing songs while lighting bonfires. In Germany, they dress up like it's Halloween, play pranks on people, and cause all sorts of noisy raucousness to scare evil spirits away.

Like so many things I've learned about the occult, Walpurgis is confusing. Walpurgis features villages where witches chant and dance around bonfires on one hillside, while effigies of witches are burned in large pyres on the other. What a creepy mix of witch-love with witch-hate. But that sort of fits Melanie, doesn't it? Melanie wants to use her witchcraft to hunt witches. Still, the creepiest thing to me is that this little demon-girl seemed to perfectly understand the holiday while I had to research it all morning in the library.

"Hello, Liam."

It's a familiar voice. Cline is wearing thick black gothic lipstick, and her lips and face are emotionless. She's wearing black suspenders over a white T-shirt. Her dark hair is short, and her eyebrows are shaved. A large bald, broad-shouldered man stands beside her. He is pale with a large shaggy blond beard and is wearing all black with purple shades. I recognize him as Kurt, the male leader of their cult.

"Ninety-three," Kurt says with a solemn nod.

Whatever the hell that means.

"How is she?" Cline asks, deadpan.

"In a lot of pain," I say, closing the book. "What can I do to save her?"

"Help us kill the girl," replies Cline with a shrug.

"Silvia and I returned to Alabama," Kurt says. "The house was abandoned. You guys called the cops? Well, it wouldn't be surprising if the place was condemned after the body of her father was discovered. And with both girls dabbling in occult witchcraft, they probably were sent to a funny farm. But sanatorium or not, we have to find her. We can use divination. If we do that, you can help. Knowing what she did to our god, she's probably not only after your unborn child, she probably plans on killing your wife. Your wife is, after all, the leader of your order too."

"Melanie hunts witches," I reply.

"Have you been invoking the Ritual of the Pentagram?" asks Cline, nodding.

"And the Lesser Ritual of the Hexagram," I reply with a nod. "Yes, I've studied your rituals."

Cline smiles at Kurt. I think it's one of the only times I've seen her smile.

"We don't have the doctor," Cline says, "but we have you,

witch. And we have your book. You cast with your Book of Shadows and lead your coven, and it might be enough to send this abomination into the fire. We propose summoning the girl astrally in your backyard during ceremony. There we can trap her once and for all."

"But can we get rid of the Ekimmu while still leaving the girl unharmed?"

"That girl murdered Luminous!" Kurt rages. "She even killed her own father. Possession or not, Melanie's mind is diseased. Maybe brilliant, but seriously fucked up in the head. And now this little piece of shit is preparing to kill your—"

"Meet me at my house tomorrow for ceremony."

"Does Alondra know about us casting at your house?" Cline asks.

"She's too sick."

2

SITRA ACHRA

"Tonight under the blessed stars of Astraeus, upon the trees of Cernunnos, by the light of Gaia and the magic of Hecate, we congregate as a united circle. Once more, our two circles meet as one." Alondra wrote these words in my book, *Broomstick*, when she prepared her eulogy for Lucius. I'm reading my wife's words to the Abaddon Order again— while perspiring. It's hot as hell on this humid summer evening. And despite the pleasant smell of the forest mixed with the burning embers in our cackling fire in my backyard glade, these flames are sure not helping quell this heat.

Rachel nods to my left, and Bill nods to my right. They're both hooded in black cloaks. Rachel's bright gold hair glows yellow in the firelight. Bill's grown a goatee, like my thin beard, which is growing out now. There are a few more black-robed witches near us, but the majority of the attendees tonight are on the other side of the fire wearing scarlet.

"We preside among friends," I continue, "but tonight is bittersweet."

I take a deep breath and shut the book.

"You all know why we're here. My wife is sick. Silvia and

I witnessed the possession of the girl in Alabama. That little demon-freak admitted to attacking your leader. She killed Lucius. We're up against a powerful force. I saw this girl conjure pouring rain inside her house and then drag Agnes along the ceiling of her living room. This is Agnes, mind you, our headmaster and witch leader, the most powerful witch in the world."

"It's possible Alondra isn't sick because of Melanie, Liam," interjects Rachel.

I turn around and look back at my house. All the lights are off, including those on my outdoor patio, but from our backyard, under the half moonlight, I can make out the large floor-to-ceiling window of the upstairs bedroom. Alondra is up there, in pain.

"Our order doesn't ascribe much power to you witches," says one of the red-robed males. "The possessed girl's spell-casting causing your so-called powerful witch leader to fly around a room doesn't impress us. The demon-possessed freak could do it to anyone not schooled in hermeticism."

"Doesn't matter," Kurt objects. "Liam and Silvia said the girl admitted to attacking the doctor. That's all we need to know. Liam, whether she hurt your wife or not, the girl is guilty. And we are here to punish her."

"That's why we're here," I reply with a nod.

"We've already sent curses, guys," Silvia says. "It hasn't hurt that little freak yet."

"That girl killed Lumi, Nancy!" cries a female stranger. "Lumi! I mean, god, as far as I'm concerned—"

"Terry, I know!" Silvia shouts back. "I know! Fuck, I was there, okay! I'm saying *we* haven't gotten to the kid, that's all, dummy. I brought you all here to Hawthorne to change that with Liam's coven."

"Show me this child's home and I'll bleed her," says another man. "That's far simpler than their witchcraft."

"We have the address," says Kurt. "The beast is residing at a relative's home in Montgomery. It's true, Silvia, that there is no evidence that our curses haven't touched her yet. Androgyne watches. The girl is alive and well. And so, tonight, we change all that."

"We intend to use divination by witch flames." Cline folds her arms, nodding to everyone in the group across from me.

Silvia once told me that Kurt was their leader. I don't think so. I think this woman has led the group ever since Lucius died.

"The girl's a witch, so we will attack her with witchcraft. With the help of your coven, Liam, and your book, we will manifest the girl in your fire and burn her to death."

"But what makes you think they can help?" asks another male member, laughing. "Half their members are on break from studying. Alondra's coven is a circle of students."

"Stop fighting them," says another woman. "Their leader wants to stop this girl more than we do. His wife's sick."

"And I don't doubt his power," interjects Cline. "Silvia told me of Liam's spellcasting. Plus he has the book. One of the doctor's lifelong dreams was to find his grimoire. He told me that was the whole reason he came here to America. As far as I'm concerned, the decision's made. We're here to cast magic with witches tonight. With your casting last Ostara, witches, you united with us. In the same respect, tonight we will honor your High Priestess and come together once more." She turns to a girl beside her. "Darbie, present our gift to their High Priest."

"I don't trust witches," says yet another male member, spitting by his side. "They spend more time fucking under moonlight than casting real magic."

Some red-cloaked witches laugh.

"*Enough!*" cries Kurt, jumping up. He removes his robe

and throws it to the side. Now he's wearing only shorts under his thick, shaggy golden beard. "Tonight, we are two pillars made stronger under moon worship!"

Then he grabs a short sword lying on the grass. Not knowing his ways, I fear he's going to charge someone with the ceremonial sword. Instead, he slashes the blade in the air, chanting something under his breath while creating swooshing sounds with the blade.

He steps in one direction, recites gibberish, and then turns and slashes in another. I recognize a few words from the Qabalah. Then I hear the names of biblical angels. He's obviously performing their Ritual of the Pentagram—though a far more aggressive and violent version than any I've ever studied.

After making a full circle, he thrusts the sword into the grass and kneels before me. Then breathing heavily, glaring into my eyes, appearing ready to tear me apart, he says, "We follow the law, brother." He bows his head deeply. "Ninety-three. Ninety-three. Ninety-three."

And he bows his head again.

Silvia strikes a small handheld metal drum, making a tone like a bell.

Slowly, Kurt rises, walks around the fire, and then sits back down across from me. But he doesn't avert his intense gaze from me.

"We present our order's wand as a gift to you, Liam," says Cline, standing and gesturing to the red-cloaked woman named Darbie. "Normally it is given to initiates, but you have already ascended the Qabalistic cross and passed D'at by trauma because of that filth. So we offer this as a weapon against our common adversary. Darbie, present your wand to him."

Darbie removes her hood. Like Cline, her eyebrows are shaven, but Darbie has a shaved head and darker skin. She takes a long, thin wand from a pocket in her robe. Then she walks all the way around the bonfire. Beside me, she drops on one knee, like Kurt did. She presents the long black stick to me with both extended hands.

"This is my wand," Darbie says, gazing deeply into my eyes. "Shaped by sculpting holly wood from the holly tree. From base to zenith, I focus my intent and direct my magic along the four cardinal directions in the plane of illusion we call Kenoma. Blessed Androgyne offers my wand to you as lead wizard of your clan. Do you accept my gift from our order?"

I take the wand with a nod.

"Hail Satan," Darbie says quietly with a smile, bowing deeply again.

"Hail Satan," murmur the others.

Kurt leaps up, slashes his sword through the air once more, and dances around the bonfire.

And the bell is struck again.

I remember that when I met Lucius, their leader, he once called magic *theater*. Well, the way Kurt's dancing about and Darbie's carrying on, now I get why.

"Present the chalice," Kurt says, panting. "Fill the cup under the temple of blessed Sophia. Tonight, we are the guests of moon worship. We partake in moon magic through your goddess, Hecate. As said by blessed Androgyne, we shall use witchcraft to battle witchcraft. Drink from our cup, wizard. In our order, our doctor used special herbs to reach a higher astral plane. But, being your guests, we will partake in your witch brew tonight."

The bell tolls again. Then Silvia nods to Rachel.

Rachel stands up. She walks behind me. But then...she hesitates.

"Liam," she says, cocking her head back, "are you sure Alondra is okay with this?"

Rachel's not concerned if we drink mandragora. Unlike me, she's taken mandrake a dozen times before. I think she's worried we're practicing a ritual with strangers—and without Alondra.

I lie with a nod. It's not like I can ask her right now.

The bell tolls again.

One of their ladies in red gives Rachel a very large silver chalice. Rachel opens a small wooden barrel and pours our mandragora into the chalice.

Then I look back at the large-windowed upstairs bedroom again. I sat with Alondra up there for a couple hours after dinner. She was shaking in bed, groaning in pain for hours.

"You still want me to run the ceremony, man?" Bill whispers, touching my shoulder.

"You know the words better than me, Bill."

Rachel hands me the chalice, now filled with red, sticky goo. By the flickering flames, it doesn't look much different from blood.

Then Darbie walks around the fire and stands behind the flickering bonfire right across from me. Eyebrow-less and bald, she looks creepy in the firelight.

She bows.

"Drink, High Priest," Darbie says, gesturing toward my cup. "Drink. Drink and you shall be reborn. Blessed are you that feels the energy of the eternal maker of our firmament —blessed Sophia. Let her magic course through your body. With the help of herbs, this circle, this fire, your blood, and now my wand, unite tonight as we amplify our mutual intent. As above, so below. As below, so above. Drink, wizard, drink. And dissolve into the blessed knowing."

The cup shakes in my hands.

"Lee," Bill says, tapping my shoulder. "It'll be fine, man."

3

____

THE EFFIGY

Kenosha sits in her green robe across from the bonfire. Agnes sits beside her in her blue cloak. And Alondra is next to me, smiling. We're meeting in my backyard to try to rid me of my Ekimmu demon possession. There's no other way I'd be crazy enough to ever attend one of their witch ceremonies.

~

"You're burning him! My God! Stop this, Cadence! You must! Stop it now! You're hurting Bill!"

"Devil."

~

I taste a horrible bitter taste. So I throw up.

~

"Whenever and wherever I fail, I ask God to forgive me. Forgive my sins, for they are as numerous as the stars in the heavens, but my love is as eternal as the waves upon the sea. Agape. Agape. Agape."

Scarlet robes fade in and out of focus. The red seems to be part of the flames. Alondra once told me that our magic worships the moon, while theirs worships the sun. Seeing red beside flickering yellow light makes me feel as if I, indeed, am facing the sun.

I rub my eyes.

Rachel looked so serious and worried before. Now she's running naked around the fire, laughing, bucking up and down like a steer, spitting fire into everyone's face. Long horns have grown from her head. They're like stag horns. But like a dragon, she spits flames into everyone's face. No one screams or runs. I'm laughing. Because, I mean, come on, it's obviously not real fire.

I disrobe.

"*Revelare*," I say, pointing my black wand at the fire. "*Revelare*, Melanie. Reveal yourself."

"Burn the witch," says Kurt.

"Kiss me."

Silvia stands naked, gazing up into my eyes.

"Kiss me."

She embraces me tightly, her pale, naked breasts pressing against my bare chest. Her long golden hair shines in half moonlight. I gaze down at my naked body and my erect cock.

"Love me," she repeats with a giggle. She closes her eyes and licks her lips. "Kiss and love me. We are one. Kiss my lips, High Priest. Kiss me."

"I'm married, Silvia," I say with a chuckle.

But I put my head on her shoulder. And my hands can't avoid groping her soft skin, on her back and down her legs.

"I'm so worried, Silvia," I say, squeezing her more tightly. "I'm so scared." Tears fall from my eyes. Silvia runs her tongue along my cheek, licking my tears.

"Me too, Lee," Alondra whispers in my ear. "God, it hurts so bad, babe."

Silvia runs her fingers through my hair, and her lips touch mine gently.

"Be calm," Silvia whispers in my ear. "Blessed are you that feels the energy of the eternal. And now, let our magic course through your veins. Now that we're free to do as we please, I invite you to lie with me by the fire tonight. Take me. Come and be with me. Make love to me. It will enhance our magic. That's what your friend and I did. Remember? The circle will become one in our sex. Ceremonial tantra can fix everything happening to your wife. Can't it?"

"That's not funny, Silvia. I love my wife."

"Your friend made love to me," Silvia whispers, gazing into my eyes. "It bound us as one, together in love. Why can't you love me too?"

"You're my friend."

"Your friend was my friend. My friends are your friends. We are all friends under fire. I am woman. You are man. Break the chains. This world is made of man and woman, yin and yang, ones and zeros. Two pillars. Take me and embrace me. And fuck me. Do you smell it? Our sex. Don't you feel it? That's wet. Earthy. Muddy. Abaddon. Abandon. Abaddon. Ground, wind, fire, water. Love... Embrace and make love by the flames for the sake of others so that we may finally die alive. Let death cast out our alchemy and join together our very souls before this fire tonight. Together, all for the sake of your eternal married life."

"No, Silvia. No."

But I feel her running her fingers down my legs. Every time her hand draws close to my cock, I lurch back.

"Stop it, Silvia," I say with a laugh.

The flames of red and orange light dance along the trees of the surrounding forest. It's not our bonfire. Thick cords of light are coming down and entwining into large strings. These cords are the width of the tree trunks, but as bendable as strings, plasma flying around in darkness, celebrating the union of our energies in knotted ecstasy. And everything spins around my focal center, and wherever I look I see shapes. Red, green, and blue figures in the shapes of triangles, stars, circling my forest glade. I understand that these figures—lines, triangles, squares, and circles—create everything. And all is climaxed by the sex of our whispers. And our mystical humming. The whispers appear in every crack and crevice, on the ground, on the bark, in all the gaps between tree branches, along Silvia's soft skin, and in every opening on her body, the body of our circle, within and without her, and before and after, all time.

"*Lux tenebris*," Bill says commandingly.

"*Lux tenebris*," says the group, in trance.

Bill's naked body faces our bonfire, and he is raising an athame in his left hand. His lips twitch and his eyes are open wide, facing flickering fire. For he, like me, drank from the silver chalice.

I stare into the fire.

"We anoint ourselves in black magic," Bill says. "Abaddon. We are witches among guests tonight. Follow our way, newcomers, for you are on Hawthorne's hallowed ground now."

"We follow."

"Repeat the words of darkness then," Bill says with a nod. "*Lux tenebris. Lux tenebris. Lux tenebris. Circulo. Satana.*"

"*Lux tenebris. Lux tenebris. Lux tenebris. Circulo. Satana.*"

"*Hoc circulo, Satana,*" Bill says. He grins at me and nods. "*Hoc circulo.* In wisdom, I ask for guidance by the light bearer of the East. Lucifer. Morning star. Venus. *Hoc circulo. Lucifer. Lucifer. Satana.* As I feel the power of mandragora course through my veins, I invoke the power of Hecate, goddess of witchcraft. I ask for a dual torch to light each column. Invoke the abomination here and now within our fire. *Revelare.* Show the abomination, so that we may smite the earthen element. Oh mighty ones, reveal filth in the flames of this Hawthorne bonfire tonight before you. *Revelare.*"

I stare at the fire, directing my wand and focusing all my intent.

A figure appears! A small black witch's robe stands in the center of our large burning bonfire. The flames are as tall as a person, but the robe is small, small enough to fit a child. There's no struggle. Because nobody's inside the robe. It's just Melanie's small black robe, as if hanging on a stick, burning. The robe is like a statue, motionless, with only the fabric of the robe fluttering in the flames, but it still feels evil, reminding me of the still Ekimmu demons. The stillness feels unsettling. This burning of her robe feels like... well, I suppose, like an *effigy.* Sort of like the effigies of witches in bonfires on Walpurgis Night.

"*Revelare! Revelare! Revelare!*"

There is a flash of brilliant white light. The white light remains, making me squint.

Then, slowly, things become clear.

4
—————

THE FOOL

"*Ouroboros. Shed your tail and leave my hallowed* ground. Viper, leave in peace. I am the Hawthorne Witch. *Spiritus. Spiritus. Spiritus.*"

The white light brightens more and more. As my eyes slowly adjust, I find myself in the center of a wild, grassy field surrounded by trees under bright yellow sunlight. I...I haven't moved. This is my backyard!

The yellows and greens in Alondra's backyard are vibrant in the bright white light. Every leaf is translucent, a chartreuse color, shining as the sunlight passes through every leaf and blade of grass. The forest, which was dark and foreboding, now reflects a golden hue in the sunlight. There's even a glow in the fine particles of dust in the air.

I turn to my house. Painted white, it reflects brighter than ever, shining like alabaster stone. The large bedroom window seems to reflect like a bright mirror. Birds chirp. Leaves stir. And the fresh air smells only of leaves and grass. Gone is that burning smell. I feel the opposite of what I felt before. I feel at peace.

"Shed your tail and leave, devil. Do not disturb my

hallowed ground. I am the Hawthorne Witch. *Spiritus. Spíritus. Spiritus.*"

There, at the center of our wild, grassy glade, before a pile of old logs—our extinguished bonfire—sits a young woman, cross-legged, wearing one of our black robes. Alondra? I've seen my wife sit like this in meditation in our backyard. Walking closer, I find the woman staring intensely at a book by her side: my book, *Broomstick.* She's whispering to herself. No...humming. I've seen Alondra do this, too, in concentration. But no, this isn't Alondra. Allie is about her age though. The lady's eyes are shadowed in black, and her fingers and neck are adorned in gold and silver. Her lips are black. She has long dark hair like Allie, but darker skin.

"*Ouroboros,*" the woman repeats almost in a whisper. "Shed your tail and leave my hallowed ground."

I just stand over her. I don't know for how long. It could be seconds, minutes, maybe an hour. But I just stand. Because everything feels good around here. Everything. I feel so much peace. It's how I imagine heaven.

Tears pool in my eyes. I don't know why, but the tranquility makes me sad.

I fall to my knees.

Is it from lack of sleep? Worry? Whatever happens after our ritual, my wife could die. And even if Alondra doesn't die, she may lose our child. All the strain of the past week seems to weigh heavily enough on me to make me break down, because, I think, I feel unburdened around this stranger. Her sense of ease is juxtaposed to and backward from everything I feel inside.

"I'm lost."

She stops humming.

"Please, stop hurting her," she says quietly.

"Who?"

"My friend."

She looks up. Her eyes aren't mesmerizing, like other witches'; they're brown and innocent.

"A witch is attacking us," I say, shaking my head. "We have to do something. A girl that threatens the life of my wife and child, and our friends."

The woman just smiles. Then, slowly, she moves her hand along her black robe. The sound of the fabric brushing over her arm seems loud amid the silence. Her movements are precise, fluid, as if she's performing a magic trick. From her right sleeve she takes out a card. She lays the card on the green grass. I recognize it as an arcana card from the tarot deck. It's an image of a man walking carelessly one step away from plummeting over a cliff. This is called "The Fool" card.

"*Il matto*," she says, nodding slowly. "You cannot cast shadows in darkness, Father. Lead a demon to harm, and the demon shines darkness back upon you. The Wicca witch knows this."

"I only see a witch threatening me."

She shakes her head. Then she reaches under her sleeve again, pulling out a second card. This one is the grim reaper. She lays the "Death" arcana card beside "The Fool" before her lap.

"*La Morte*," she says, gazing at both cards now. "Change in you? But I feel only dark witchcraft. Indeed, death. Too much grounding leads to mud. If you insist we are dust, father, then to dust you go. You cannot shade darkness. Just as you cannot burn light. If there is darkness upon darkness upon darkness upon darkness upon darkness upon darkness, what do you think you create? Choose one path and the other, and stand forth in the center. You cannot find your way by one path alone."

But I shake my head. I don't understand.

Very rapidly, she chops her hands through the air,

reminding me of Kurt's swordplay, as if her hands are ceremonial swords. This sudden brisk movement feels jarring amid the tranquility. Yet her moves are smooth, like a dancer's. Her limbs move so fast that they lose focus and her arms blend together, as if she has more than two arms. Returning into focus, she runs two left fingers along the dirt and grass, while reaching high with her right arm, pointing two fingers up to the cerulean sky above.

She presents an empty left hand before me. Then she turns the hand upside down and turns her palm back up. Now lying in her left palm is a large silver crucifix. It's as if she's performing another magic trick. She closes her eyes and presses the crucifix tightly against her chest, still pointing two fingers of her right hand toward the sky.

"I gave my body and soul to my lord, Jesus Christ. Who do you give yourself to? Either left or right, down or up, earth or air, fire or water, all perennial paths lead the same way. What perennial path do you live by?"

"I am lost."

"Mother taught only right-sided magic. She did this to fight the evil you sowed. But had she believed in balance from the start, I really don't think I ever would have had to come here to Hawthorne."

"Who are you?"

"I am the Hawthorne Witch," she says with a gentle smile. "My name is Cadence. As you continue to play with dirt, you form mud. *Malkuth*. I ask once more, what path do you follow, Father? *Qlippoth? Belial?* Vanity? Venus? If you are truly lost, then leave. Those that choose to create confusion in this world multiply shadows. By the left, I prophesy great suffering. By the right, you can be my light. This is not because you choose only the left. It is because you follow nothing right."

And then she actually laughs.

"I don't understand."

"*Il matto,*" she says, still laughing. "*Il matto.* Ask yourself when your head becomes clear. My friend once taught me that—" She looks up at me, squinting. "When there's imbalance in this world, darkness can be cast out by light. Just as light can be covered. But neither ever leaves us. If you look too far west, all joy that remains is pain."

"Who told you this?"

"Melanie." Then she returns to staring forward. "Please stop hurting her, Liam. Every time you hurt Melanie, you hurt Hawthorne. Open your eyes and see the evil you and Alondra are casting."

"I don't understand."

"Leave me then, devil."

Oh, Liam. Liam, if you only could have just left her in peace.

5

AGAPE

"Darkness fades to light. Shadow by fire. Lux tenebris. Lux alba. Left into right. Right into left. Columned by black, columned by white. Eleven. Eleven. As below, so above. As above, so below. Please reveal my shadow so that I may find peace. Shine the light upon daemons and free me from chains. Allay all suffering from all souls. Shadows, though I know you are eternal, I cast your energy away from my hallowed, hollowed heart. In return, I wish to fill this vessel with light. Because now I see darkness. And now I know pain. Whenever and wherever I fail, I ask God to forgive me. Forgive my sins, for they are as numerous as the stars in the heavens, but my love is as eternal as the waves upon the sea."

"It's no use saying all those fancy words, Katie. You're not gonna ever be changing that man's mind, now, forever and ever more."

"I have to try, Melanie. For them and you. I just have to try."

"Now, don't you be worrying yourself over me."

"Because we're friends?"

"We sure are, Cadence Hawthorne. The best of friends."

Agape... Agape. Agape.

6

AND THEN SHE SCREAMS

The bonfire at the center of my backyard flashes into my vision. And all that darkness returns. But the flames are growing higher than ever now. All the witches and wizards are disrobed, rushing around it, bobbing heads up and down, laughing and crying, circling around and around me by the fire, faster and faster at unnatural speed. It's dizzying. Sickening. The air no longer smells fresh and pleasant. It's suffocating, nauseating, filled with the foul smell of urine mixed with mud. All the while, white ash falls from the sky. These white flakes slowly blanket the grass like snow. And the fire burns unbearably hot, making these imitation snowflakes seem that much more perverse.

Sweat drips down my back and blurs my eyes.

I still make out the small robe, Melanie, or her black effigy, burning in our pyre. Only now I hear her screaming. And no matter how much I want to heal my wife, the little girl's suffering is absolutely intolerable.

"Stop!"

The pace of the dancers slows. But they still encircle me.

"Lucifer!" Bill counters. "Morning star. Lead us. Amicus. Amica. *Hoc circulo. Lucifer. Lucifer. Satana. Adramelch! Beleth! Marduk! Paimon! Balam! Belial!*"

Melanie screams again.

"*Stop!*" I shout, pointing my wand at the flames. "*Stop it! I command this conjuring to stop. All of you, stop it now! Everyone, stop moving!*"

Everyone freezes. Not just everyone, everything.

It seems even the leaves in the forest have stopped stirring. Two witches, Silvia and Cindy, are holding hands with their torsos lurching back, their lips frozen in a devilish grin. Others are still, eyes wide, just blankly staring into nothing, as if mad. Others seem lost, having stopped mid-step while wandering around our bonfire. Only the fire continues to crackle and flame, and it is still snowing ash.

It's as if I paused a movie. Or has time itself stopped?

An owl is frozen in midair right above me. Seeing an owl is rare enough, but this bird is covered in dripping, frozen blood. I marvel that the bird is midflight and yet perfectly still.

"*Stop!*"

The owl bursts into flames, becoming a ball of fire. It burns brightly until it is extinguished into ash. More ash. This ash mixes with the white ash raining down on us. Now so much ash has fallen that blankets of white flakes cover our feet.

"*Stop hurting her, Liam!*" shouts Cadence's disembodied voice. "*Stop the spell now!*"

Melanie screams again.

"*Stop!*" I shout. "*Stop the spell!*" I hold my book aloft before the fire. "*Stop this curse upon my hallowed ground. I command all of you! Stop! Stop everything! Prohibe! Prohibe! Prohibe!*"

Melanie's cries are replaced by Alondra's. My wife's

agony is heard coming from the house behind me. And with it, the freezing ends. Everyone stirs, now staring back toward the house. Alondra screams again. That makes me abandon everyone and rush indoors.

7

SHE'S GONE

Sitting on our fuchsia couch in front of the big-screen TV in my living room, I'm watching a Braves game. I really can't care. I mean, I love baseball more than anything in the world, but not much can make me smile anymore.

I rub my eyes.

I haven't been sleeping much either. Uncle Hanley, Alondra's dad, is sitting in our lounge chair by the sliding glass door. His head is turned toward the television too. I think he told me once he doesn't really care for baseball.

There's shouting upstairs. That's not my wife, that's Mom.

God, after that terrifying night at the Grants' house and that freak-girl, I can't stop thinking that all of Alondra's pain is that little monster's fault.

"Your wife is one tough egg to crack." Uncle Hanley forces a smile. "Yep, she sure is. She sure is. She's a lot like her mom, Liam. Which now sounds a lot like *your* mom." He actually laughs. "Reckon that won't be the last of the yells coming from upstairs. Those two are both tough women."

"It's been so hard this past month, Uncle Hanley," I say with a nod. "It's been so difficult. Just thanks for coming."

He nods.

"It's not why we got married."

"Huh?" he asks, scratching his head. "Whatcha say there, Liam?"

"Alondra and I didn't get married because she got pregnant," I reply. "I love her. It's just that—"

"Now why would you say that? I can tell you two have loved one another ever since I first met you. Don't be thinking bad thoughts now, son. You got enough difficult things on your mind right now."

Well, that's for sure.

"Her pain died down after last night," I say. "Thank God for that."

"I think she's going to be all right," Uncle Hanley says. "If the two of them upstairs don't kill each other."

"*You stubborn girl!*" cries Mom upstairs. "*I should call an ambulance and be done with all of this! You think you're the only one suffering here!*"

"*Now I know where Lee gets his temper!*" Allie shouts back. "*Go! Do it! Go call an ambulance! I won't go, Mom. You'll have to drag me out of my house!*"

I hear rushing down the stairs. Mom freaks out Sheba, and our black cat comes barreling into the living room and jumps into my arms.

"*Liam!*" cries Mom. "*Liam!*"

"We're in the living room, Mom," I say, heaving a sigh.

"Oh, Lee," Mom says. Then she grins at Uncle Hanley. "Oh, hello. I didn't know you were here. I... Lee, why didn't you call a doctor these past few weeks? You told me you haven't slept, and the whole time she's been in pain? Alondra's in terrible straits. You waited too long. She's so sick."

"My daughter doesn't believe in doctors, Christine," Uncle Hanley says with a chuckle. But then he runs his hand through his thin hair. "Nope. She doesn't care much for medicine."

"Either of you should have taken her to the hospital. That girl is still hurting terribly. Pain this bad could have been controlled with medicine. You know my job is in the ICU. I know she could be getting through this much better with some morphine. Having her suffer like this—"

"But the boy tried, Chrissy," Uncle Hanley says, heaving a sigh. "He tried. And I believe him. When my daughter's mind's made up, there's just no way of changing it. She's stubborn like an ox. She won't do anything against her will. Why, this is so hard on him because—"

"But that's why I'm mad! Not only is she in pain, she messed up my son, Mr. Hanley! All for nothing. All Alondra needed to do was be seen in a hospital for a D and C and be done with this whole thing. She's hurting so terribly, but she's not letting anybody help her. I tell you, I spoke with her, that imbecile upstairs—"

"You never liked her," I snap. "You've been cold to her, Mom, ever since you first met her at our house."

She shakes her head and throws up her hands. Then she plops down on the other side of the couch. She looks at the baby blue pillow and shakes her head. I don't think Mom cares for my wife's eclectic taste either—she just hasn't had a chance yet to comment about the furniture.

"That's not true," she says. "That's just not true, Liam. It's not that I don't like her. It has nothing to do with her. I like her, all right." Then she looks at Uncle Hanley. He nods. "Oh, I just don't like her temperament. Your daughter's something else. Too strong-willed. But I know what you see in her, Liam. I get that. I also know how much you love one another. It...it doesn't matter what the hell I think now, does it?"

She folds her arms and stares at the television. Mom doesn't like baseball either.

"We think the baby will be all right with just natural remedies," I reply.

My mom lurches back on the sofa. Then she stares at me. She seems to lose all her anger, slowly shaking her head.

"Oh, Lee," she says, shaking her head. "Sweetheart. Lee, there's...nothing... I'm sorry. Honey, didn't your wife tell you about all her bleeding?"

"Yes."

"Liam, Alondra's bleeding a lot. That's why she's so weak. She's had a miscarriage. I'm... I'm sorry, but there's not going to be a baby. Not now. She told me she thinks she got pregnant nearly three months ago. That's really too late for this to go naturally. That's why she's having such a hard time. But she said she's seen a lot of blood, and the pain is going down. Thank God. But...I still think you should take her to a doctor. For *her* sake. Not for any baby's. As far as a baby, Lee, you're just not going to have one. Not now."

"Well..." Uncle Hanley says. "Well." He takes a deep breath. "Well..." God, I don't think there's anything worse than seeing one of the most jovial men I've ever met look unhappy.

Uncle Hanley just turns back to the TV screen. Then he folds his hands under him, closes his eyes, and mutters, "The sufferings of this present time are not worthy to be compared with the glory which shall be revealed to us. Amen."

Mom jumps up in a huff. She heads to our sliding glass door and looks out at the backyard. She doesn't open the door. She just stares at the porch and our forest glade under the evening sky.

"We did some things," I say. "Kind of...like doctor things. I thought it would have made sure the baby would be okay."

Mom just slowly shakes her head.

"Talk to her, Liam," Mom says, still gazing outside. "I'm sorry. Alondra will tell you. The baby's gone."

8

MY WIFE

THE SUN SHINES BRIGHTLY THROUGH THE LARGE WINDOW OF our bedroom, lighting up the whole room. It will be another clear and warm summer day in Hawthorne. I'm sitting with my back to the window on a lounge chair across from the bed. I didn't sleep. I couldn't. Not with Allie moaning all night. I offered to hold her, but that just seemed to make the groans worse. And now, though finally sleeping, she's shivering like crazy.

My eyes drift to the digital clock on our nightstand. It reads nine-eleven in the morning.

She squints her eyes open but turns away from the open window.

"Hi."

"Hey, Allie. Can I get you anything?"

She shakes her head. But then she puts her hand over her eyes. "Actually, close the drapes, won't you? It's so bright outside."

I get up and close our large curtains. But then it seems too dark. So I walk over to our adjoining bathroom and turn on the bathroom light.

"You want to go back to sleep?" I ask, sitting on the bed beside her. I slowly run my fingers through her long hair. There are wrinkles under her tired eyes, and she seems even paler than usual this morning.

She takes my hand and kisses the back of it. Then she shakes her head.

"I'm so sorry I fought with your mom," she says with a woeful grin.

"Wasn't the first time. She's tough, like you. When you're well, I'm sure you two will straighten everything out."

"I'm not so sure. I don't think she ever really cared for me much."

"Well," I say, leaning down and kissing her lips. "I'm absolutely crazy about you."

"My husband," she says with a nod, kissing the back of my right hand again. She tries to straighten up in bed, but I gently lay her head back down on the pillow.

"Just rest."

"Lee, I told your mom about the baby. I'm sorry, babe, our baby's gone... It's funny, I'd heard about how sad people get over miscarriages. Diana, in our circle, had a miscarriage. You never met Diana, she was with Jane and me before she graduated a couple years ago. The coven tried to save her baby too, but we couldn't. Diana was so miserable. I didn't get it then. But boy, do I get it now. But you know...that sorrow is covered up because nobody seems to want to talk about it. Nobody knows just how painful the ordeal is, especially with ours being just far enough along for me to show. Maybe it's my fault for believing a baby would come no matter what. I mean, Rachel and the whole gang were so excited. Funny, I even thought I predicted a girl's birth." She laughs. "Somehow...I was certain we had a daughter somewhere in our future. But, I mean, you guys even ran a ceremony to protect her. Right?"

"You knew about the ceremony?"

"I saw you casting around the fire outside through the window," she says. "And all their red robes."

"We had a ceremony with the Abaddon Order."

She nods.

"Do you think that was a bad idea?"

"I would have done the same thing."

"It was intense. But I ended up stopping the ceremony when I thought Melanie was getting hurt. And that's when we heard you hurting. God...I almost wonder if I traded Melanie's life for our baby's."

"No. I was in pain after the miscarriage. After all that bleeding, the baby was gone way before your ritual."

"I didn't want to hurt Melanie. But I also wanted to help you. But, honestly, Allie, I think if I knew for sure that it would be either Melanie or you, I would have let the kid die."

Alondra nods.

"Sounds like you did the right thing, Lee. I told you I don't think we should go after that poor girl anymore. I think we should leave her family alone. I don't know, but...I don't believe Melanie caused any of it. I was fine for weeks after getting back from her house. I don't think it's her fault. I think, God, I think the way we left that little girl in that house was absolutely horrible enough."

"Forget all of that now." I run my hand through her hair. I lean down and kiss her cheek. "Don't worry about anything, Alondra."

She nods. But then she shivers again.

So I move the top sheets over her.

"Should I get more Tylenol?" I ask. "Mom said it'd help your shivers. You're still shaking."

"I'm not shaking from cold, Liam. It hurts."

"More reason for Tylenol," I say, jumping up.

But she snatches my wrist. "Forget it. Do you...Lee, do you think we're going to be okay?" She forces a smile. Then she squeezes my hand real tight. "Something feels wrong. I don't know. Not just me being sick. Something just feels off here now."

And that really scares me. Because I've never known Alondra to be unsure about anything.

"What could be wrong?" I lie with a shrug. "I married the love of my life."

"Me too," she says and kisses my hand again. "But...I'm not so sure we're going to have a kid now. I was so sure we were. I think that hurts the most. Somehow, I don't see any baby in our future now."

And that sounds awful. She lets go of my hand.

If Alondra were someone who cries, I'm pretty sure she'd cry now. But I've hardly ever seen her cry. She winces instead, touching her stomach again.

"You okay?"

"It does this from time to time."

"Allie, I have to tell you about something that happened in the ceremony. Something good. I saw something in a vision after taking mandrake. A vision that was real good. Actually, I think you prophesied it all correctly. I do think we are going to have a daughter. I saw her in trance."

"I just told you we won't," she says with a chuckle.

I intertwine her fingers with mine. Then, with my other hand, I touch the small emerald in the necklace I recently gifted her.

"The sun was bright," I say, leaning close and kissing her cheek. "Everything was flooded in this amazing light. I felt so happy. And this woman was in the center of our backyard on the wild grass wearing our black robe. At first, I thought it might be you. She held the same intense focus you hold in meditation. But then I saw her face. Her features were different. She was about your age with the same long dark hair, in the same pose as you, but with brown eyes and a darker complexion. She wasn't you. But she seemed to be at such peace. She was the complete opposite of the way I felt during the ceremony around the fire. Because...God, I was so worried about everything. But, Allie, she called herself my *daughter*. She said her name was Cadence. And Cadence was the one who told me that we needed to stop hurting Melanie, just like you said. And then it was... I think it was actually this Cadence witch that helped me stop the spell.

"Then Melanie started screaming. I couldn't take a little girl screaming. Then this woman, Cadence, yelled for me to stop hurting her. So I stopped. I stopped everyone and everything. But it's like it was more because of what this witch in my vision was doing than anything I had done. It was as if this lady was there with us at the ritual, stopping the spell. Our so-called *daughter*."

Alondra smiles thinly. Then she nods, turning to the window.

"Open the drapes just a little, would you, babe?"

So I do. But this time, I'm the one squinting in the light after all the darkness in the room. Outside, yellow rays are shining on the wild green grass and between the branches of our surrounding forest. You know, our large bedroom window always provides an amazing view of the forest glade below.

"After poring through books all my life," Allie says, "it takes you, of all people, Liam, who hates witchcraft, to predict our future together. Maybe you were destined for *Broomstick* all along?"

"But am I right, Allie? Do you think my vision will come true?"

"I hope so," she says with a shrug. "I don't know. But I'll tell you one thing. If we do have a daughter, I hope she grows up to be just like her father."

9

SILVIA

IN ONE OF OUR UNIVERSITY QUADS OF CONCRETE, ARTIFICIAL lawn, and planted trees, under a huge central oak tree, there lies a secluded special mobile wagon vendor that only true Hawthorne students know of—especially now, in this awful sweaty, hot summer. But the delights it yields are popular enough to warrant this second secluded location.

I'm dressed for the heat in an old violet tie-dyed tee and black shorts. This afternoon there are lots of clouds above but no rain, making it humid. When wet, the summer weather in Hawthorne can be so intolerable. But the forecast today was that it'd be cooler. Finally. Hopefully, autumn is coming.

"That'll be a dollar," says a young girl with a smile, handing me a pretzel. She has distinctively short dark hair, a white T-shirt and shorts, and gothic black makeup. "Enjoy."

I turn to head back to the main drag on campus toward the student store—until I hear someone laughing behind me.

"Hey, Lee!" cries a voice.

I spin around and see a girl in a sleeveless white shirt, black bandana, and baggy blue jeans.

"How the hell are ya?"

"Silvia?"

Silvia's not wearing the scowl she had the last time I saw her, after I broke their curse. Their gang was so utterly pissed at me that night. Kurt looked like he wanted to thrust his ceremonial sword through my chest in the living room. I think he might have, if he hadn't left the blade back by our bonfire.

"You want me to get you a pretzel?"

She shakes her head and embraces me. Then she hooks her arm in mine—which makes me laugh—popping bubbles with the gum in her mouth as she walks with me out of the quad.

"So...where are we heading?" she asks, smacking gum.

"Well, *I'm* going to the student store. I really don't have much to do today. I thought the student store would be a cool place to run through some books for the upcoming year. I would have done it at the library, had the place not closed for construction yesterday—it'll probably be closed the rest of the year."

"I thought school was starting for you guys?"

"Brilliant timing, right? Well, coincidentally, I'm heading to the place where I met you last time you came to our college— that grassy field near the student store. Which brings up a very important question, Silvia. Why the hell are you here? Especially after you guys wanted to kill me after our last ceremony."

"First off, Liam, I told you and Lumi how much I absolutely love Hawthorne University. So what's wrong with visiting? Second, why do I ever come here to talk to you, ding-a-ling? It's always over the other thing I adore. Heavy magical stuff."

She laughs. Then she blows a big bubble by my face.

"Silvia, look—" I readjust my backpack to my other shoulder, sounding more somber. "Look, what happened in my backyard got really weird. I had a vision and a witch spoke to me using tarot. It was because of the vision of that witch, I think, that I ended the spell."

"Man, my friends are ticked off to high heaven. Cline and Kurt are, of course, beyond pissed off. All of them are shouting at me for trusting you. They hate you more than ever, Liam."

I nod.

"What cards did this witch in your vision show you?" she asks.

"The Fool and Death cards."

"Transformative," she says with a pensive nod. "But those two cards don't tell you shit. Any idiot would know you're going through a transformation. I mean, you got married and then your wife got sick. You know, I can give you a proper reading, if you want—minus the bad trip. I'm pretty good at reading cards. I can do the *I Ching* and horoscopes too. It'd be fun and totally my pleasure."

We enter the main drag of campus. Being that it's summer, it's vacant, making the width between those old brick college buildings look huge. Usually people are rushing all over the place on this walkway. So, in no time, we enter the green, grassy lawn and head up the hill toward the student store. It's a bit sloshy at the base of the hill with clear blue skies above. They must have just run sprinklers. I'm heading toward empty benches perched at the top of the hill —prime real estate when school starts.

"Also...I came to warn you."

That makes me stop halfway up the hill.

"*What is it this time!*" I cry, whirling around. She jumps

back, startled. *"I thought that cursing stuff with you and your friends was over!"*

I regret shouting at her. But, I mean...*fuck!* I can't take much more of this. I mean, really, I feel like I'm going to fucking explode.

She looks up, searching my eyes. Then her lips curl into a smile.

"Man, I'd never be angry with you. It's bitch Cline and the rest of 'em. Just as we were about to trap the beast— probably by finishing her off in your fire—you stopped the spell. You even used the wand we gifted you to do it. I think you meant well, but my friends sure didn't. If it wasn't for Alondra's cries for help, I think they would have killed you. Do you have any idea what I had to do to get them just to trust you guys and come down here in the first place? Most of us hate this town. I mean, I love it, like I told you, but they really hate it. They think it's just a bunch of stupid trees. And you know, they totally hate witches. Why did you stop our spell? Just because of some hallucination you had in a trance?"

I remove my backpack, letting it fall and plop down beside me on the grass. Then I sit down and tear off a piece of my pretzel. But I don't eat it. I just hold on to it.

Silvia gazes at me with a furrowed brow. I lean my head in my hand, heaving a sigh.

I feel her hand touch my shoulder.

"First a witch in a vision told me to, Silvia. Then I heard that kid screaming. Melanie was screaming, Silvia. Didn't you hear her? I couldn't hurt a kid."

"Oh, man...just forget it. How's Alondra?"

"We lost the baby."

"Wow, I'm sorry."

"You know, at first, she didn't even want a child. But then we loved the idea. The whole coven was so excited. We were even getting a room ready upstairs. Everyone was teasing us about our future witch baby. But now Allie's moping about the house, more depressed than I've ever seen her. She's too damn depressed to even go outside. This is Alondra, Silvia. Alondra. She's a witch all about nature. She *is* the outdoors, and she doesn't want to even step outside right now."

"Yeah, you're totally the death card. In some ways, the death card, like water, is fighting your fire element. That causes conflict. You're totally fire, Lee. Transition time is a difficult time for the soul."

"Is that my tarot reading?" I quip, looking up at her with a smirk.

She plops down beside me and pulls at some grass.

"No," she says, playing with the blades of grass. "Liam, if you're willing to cast against Melanie again, I think my friends *might* forgive you. But we have to act fast. Cline really wouldn't want me to tell you this, but... I will because you're my friend. She sent me here. That conniving bitch asked me to come to your college and find you. My friends are too proud to ask for your help. I mean, they're still so pissed off. But, even way more, they *really* want you to use your powers and hurt the girl. And they think they can do more damage against her with your book and coven than we can alone."

"Alondra and I don't want to hurt the kid. You saw the way we left the girl at the house. We already did enough damage to her." I tear off a piece of my pretzel and toss it in my mouth.

"That little devil caused your wife's miscarriage."

"There's no proof."

"You saw how much pain your wife was in at that haunted house in Alabama," she says, shaking her head. "She nearly killed your wife. Come on, Lee. You saw what that girl was doing to her."

I shake my head.

"Liam, that creepy piece of shit is a witch! A girl-witch. And she's casting. Even Agnes confirmed that. And, unlike my friends, I met Agnes, remember? I know how powerful she is, and I watched that little twerp send her flying all over the ceiling as if your headmaster were one of her toys." She gazes back down at the view of our campus. "Listen, you've got Lumi's home number, right? Lucius donated the place to Kurt and the order. We're still there. And if I'm not back in Carolina yet, someone will eventually pick up the phone. Just call me, a'ight? Cline's proud as hell, but she wants you and your book's help. The minute you want to cast with us, she'll be on board. 'Kay? And, Jeez, cheer the hell up, man. Jeez." Then she makes me laugh with her usual grimace. "Man, whatever happens, I won't ever turn on you. Not after joining with you and Bill. I'm madly in love with my two very special friends now. We're like one through ritual."

She rubs my back and pecks my cheek. She jumps up. And then she makes her way alone back down the grassy knoll toward our main drag.

"Wait, Silvia."

She cocks her head back and waves. "Bye, Lee. Love ya. Just call, okay? Or even come by again."

"Wait...Silvia, what do you mean by *joining*? I was so out of it in the ceremony. Did anything happen...between you and me that night?"

She makes me squirm by winking.

"Love ya," she says with a laugh. "Send my regards to Alondra. Tell her our proposal. I really hope your wife feels better. Blessed be, warlock. Shield or fight, we have to do something, or that little freak is just going to hurt us."

10

HER ANNIVERSARY

I park my red Camaro behind our matching antique red carriage in the long driveway and bound up our walkway. Our large white-columned antebellum manor looks tranquil this evening, at twilight under a full moon. The white light is bright, nearly brighter than our driveway and garden lighting. With all the heat this summer, I tell you, it still feels like midday.

Alondra wanted me to wait for dinner. I'm not sure why, but she's got something special planned. I'm guessing it's a celebration of the witch's holiday Mabon?

The door swings open before I can try the keyhole. I'm welcomed by a gust of wonderful artificial coolness from our air conditioner.

"Hey, Lee!" says Rachel with a nod, all smiley. She reaches out for a hug. She's wearing a denim jacket and baggy blue jeans.

"Are we having a ceremony for autumn?"

"Come in." She shakes her head. "Falconsong has a big surprise for you."

The house is dark. There's only a single hall light

upstairs. Usually before ceremony, the girls congregate in our living room. Rachel gestures to the dimly lit hallway. A flickering light is emanating from the dining room. Candles? And I smell cooked chicken.

"Go in and take a peek," Rachel adds with a wink. "I'm outsie."

"We're not celebrating Mabon?"

"Well, maybe you two are. But me and the girls are heading to Atlanta to go shopping. And maybe we'll get some dinner. We'll see. So, hi and bye. Have fun with High Priestess. You guys deserve fun together."

Then she closes the door behind her.

So I make my way along the hallway and am intercepted by Sheba. I pick up my cat and pet her. Then I turn to the dining room.

Our long dining room table is lit by, like, twenty candles, flickering along the large wooden table. Our floor-to-ceiling window seems to echo the yellow light with its reflection. There, at the head of the table, sits Alondra. She's wearing her black robe with her hood over her head. A black star is painted on her forehead. And black gothic makeup covers her eyelids and lips.

"Surprise, Liam," Alondra says with a laugh, gesturing with extended arms to the table.

There are two silver trays filled with potatoes—one mashed and another roasted—a plate of carrots and spinach, and a whole chicken, decorated with green leaf garnish, on the table. And there's a decanter full of red wine and a basket full of rolls. This is all precisely the same stuff, decorated in the same fashion, as our first meeting-dinner when I first stepped into Alondra's house two years ago.

I put Sheba down and she scurries off. Then I walk over to embrace Alondra—but she puts her hand out.

"No," she says, shaking her head. "No, you can't ruin the fun. No hugs. You didn't hug me last time."

"Are we celebrating Mabon alone?"

"No." She shakes her head. "We're celebrating *us*. We'll celebrate the holiday with the coven, at the Sabbath, later. Lee, it was two years ago today that I held a party at my house for Mabon. Do you remember? To students, it was just my back-to-school party for college. But for you and me, it was so much more. We met for the first time. You were such an adorable redhead. I think what I loved the most was seeing you sipping beer and being a wallflower on my patio, looking totally like James Dean. Do you remember? I remember. I fell in love with you that very night. I told the girls." She removes her hood, revealing her long black hair. "And it was after that, that we saw each other in our study group for Dr. Kriegel's psycho killer class. Remember? And then, well, you saw what I didn't want you to see on Hilltop Bluff. And the rest is Hawthorne University witchcraft history. So tonight I dressed up the same way that I did when Jane let you through the front door two years ago. Don't you remember all of that?"

"Of course I do, Allie."

"I really want to enjoy dinner with my favorite cute redhead again. You want to have dinner alone with me tonight, husband?"

"Sure."

"Bon appetite," she says with another giggle.

I get up and grab for her plate, but she raises her hand again. She stands and takes a knife and large fork to carve the chicken. She transfers some chicken to my plate. Then she adds potatoes.

"At least let me get the wine," I say.

"I don't think you did last time. Did you?" she asks, placing a finger on her chin. "Funny, I can't remember."

"Probably my first glass."

"Hmm," she replies with a laugh, "no, I think your first glass was when we ate here with Dad. Well, this time, you don't need to worry over all the trouble you had uncorking it, like you did with Dad. I poured the wine in the decanter."

We laugh.

"My adorable redhead," she mutters with a smile. Then she lifts up her glass for me to fill.

She lifts it in a toast to me.

I raise my glass to her.

"Did you talk with Dr. Kriegel?" I ask, sitting back down. "You said you were going to try to iron things out for your sponsorship."

"I went to the provost earlier in the week. Sure, Lee, it won't be a problem. I got into the grad program because of him." She cuts some chicken and forks it into her mouth. "Look, didn't you notice I was the only student who lectured in his class?"

"Bill sure noticed. But school's starting. Don't you need to plan with him before—"

"Don't worry about anything tonight. Tonight is our celebration. Our anniversary." And she raises her wine glass again. "Another toast. To meeting the most wonderful man I have ever met—and ever will. I love you more than anything in the world, Liam. I really do."

"I love you so much, Alondra."

And we click our crystal glasses this time. Then I get lost in those emerald eyes in the flickering light for a moment. We sip more wine. The wine is tart, but smooth. Alondra inherited a lot of money from her folks, and things like high quality wine are her forté.

And then we just eat.

But that turns awkward in the silence. It feels weird but, to be honest, it's not so unexpected with all the tension lately. Glancing back at Alondra, I can tell her smile was a ruse. She's still depressed as hell.

"Cline called me this morning," I say, forking a small potato. "She wanted to know if we're going back to Alabama with them. They said they think Melanie's returned to that demon-house. She didn't mention Silvia, even though she knows Silvia spoke to me about it on campus. I told you I saw her."

Alondra nods, chewing on a carrot.

"She just got right to the point and asked if we had made a decision about working with them again to curse Melanie. Have we?"

"I told you, I don't want to hurt the kid."

I nod.

"But it must mean a lot for them to call. They never call. They're never even available to take my calls. Lee..." She cuts more chicken but then seems to change her mind. She puts her utensils down. She swallows and pats her mouth with a white cloth napkin. "Did you ever think that maybe, just maybe, Cline's group is the one that caused all these bad things to happen to us? They've admitted over and over that they've been wanting to curse us. Isn't it possible that they're the ones making us miserable, not a little girl?"

"No," I say, shaking my head. "I really hadn't thought about that." I hadn't. It's...possible.

"Well. Do you really want to talk about all this bad stuff right now?"

"It's just Cline wants an answer, Alondra. Silvia told me she's too proud to talk to me. Well, then she called. If she's desperate enough to call now and—"

"We have no proof Melanie attacked me. The baby lived inside my belly for weeks after we came back from Alabama. I don't blame Melanie. And I'm not about to hunt her down and cast magic against her with our coven. I didn't study the arts to hurt children, Liam. True, there are bad witches in this world that seek to harm us. But they're not little kids. That cult might have lost their leader—"

"Melanie killed Lucius. Then she hurt you."

"Liam!" she snaps. But then she puts her head in her hand and shakes her head. "Did you know that I'm not even talking to Agnes or Kenosha anymore? Out of many things I regret—and I regret a bundle in my life, babe—it's what Agnes's stupid so-called council and I did to that poor girl and her family. Kenosha completely messed them up, okay? I blame Kenosha and I'll never forgive her for that. Not to mention, I blame her for cursing the love of my life. *You.* But I, damn it, I feel so upset for ruining the Grant family. So who's to blame? Kenosha? Agnes? Their lame, dumb council? Or Silvia's satanic friends from your hometown? Or is it all just a confused little girl?" And she goes back to cutting chicken. "The funny thing is, Lee, the witch council blames you and me. Can you believe that? Let it sink in. Agnes and Kenosha think we're the ones causing all this evil in Hawthorne. That's another reason I will never talk to them again."

"But Allie, whatever horrible fate has happened to that family, Melanie is still casting witchcraft against us."

"Okay," she says, throwing her silverware down on the table. "What are you going to do about it? Cline's clan wants her dead? Do you want us to go back to Geneva Forest and kill a little girl? Isn't that what you told me you stopped them from doing in our backyard?"

She glares at me with her bright emerald eyes. I look at her matching emerald pendant. It's green amid all the black of her outfit, like the Wicked Witch of the West in *The Wizard of Oz*. I remember calling her that two years ago.

But I don't want to fight.

So I sigh.

Then I hear her take a deep breath because she doesn't want to fight either. She runs her hand through her long dark hair and shakes her head. "I don't want to talk about all this right now."

"I know. I'm sorry."

She nods.

"But," I add, "there's one more thing that's been really bugging me." And then I have trouble swallowing my potatoes. This is hardly the best time, but will it ever be? And, I mean, she's already angry. "Allie, when I was in ceremony, I partook in mandragora."

"I know."

I shake my head. "It was the first time for me. And... when Silvia saw me on campus, she said something that really upset me. She said *'not after joining you and Bill'* in ritual. I know what you had Bill and her do. I saw the sex magic that you guys organized for them. But I was too out of it to know what happened between Silvia and me when you were sick. You said you saw us? Did you...do you think Silvia and I also—"

Allie's green eyes open wider than ever. She's not looking unhappy, she's looking pissed.

"Forget it," I say, raising my palm. "Forget I said anything. Dinner is wonderful. And...I think... I guess I'm ruining it."

"Yes, I think you are, Liam." But then she actually laughs. "This might be the first time in recorded history that a man is asking his wife if he was cheating on her."

"No, Allie, no, that's not what I meant."

"Okay, Lee. Well, I've seen the way Silvia looks at you. She likes you. And I have fewer hang-ups over ceremonial sex than you do. If you were to practice sex magic with her and it benefited the coven, the town, and Melanie, then— unlike you—I wouldn't mind. I'm sure that probably shocks you."

"Forget I said anything," I say, lifting my brow.

Then I scoot my chair back, jump up, and walk around the table to our floor-to-ceiling windows and gaze out at the woods, running my hand through my thin hair.

"Yes, it's possible you might have had ceremonial sex with her."

I spin around. And Alondra has a wicked grin on her face. She looks like she's on the verge of laughing. Not a mirthful laughter but one of derision and mockery. And that really pisses *me* off.

"You enjoy fighting with me, husband. We seem to fight constantly now, don't we? But that's also you. My fiery redhead wanted to fight when we met for dinner two years ago too. So you're actually reliving all of that." She chuckles. "You stood right up, gazing out the window, ready to rush out of the house, just like you are doing right now."

"I don't want to leave the house, Allie," I say, walking back around the table to my chair.

"Well, you did. But you didn't. You married me instead. So...please come back and sit down at the table with me, husband. Eat with me. Talk to me. Laugh with me. Because, love me or not, I love you to death, Liam. Always and forever and ever."

"I do love you, Allie," I say gruffly, sitting back down.

"Do you know why I dressed up like a witch tonight?"

"Because you are one. And you like to do crazy things like that just to rile me up."

"No, because you love it," she answers with a chuckle. "You fell in love with a witch because you love witches."

She pushes back her chair and stands up. Then she walks up to me, takes a knee before me, and stares up into my eyes. She runs her hand gently through my hair.

"I asked you to take the robe off last time," I say, meeting her gaze.

"No," she says with a sly grin. "I won't this time. Unless you kiss me. If you kiss me, I will. Kiss your witch, warlock."

"We didn't do that last time."

"We didn't?" she asks. She comes closer, putting her arms around my neck. "Let's do it this time. Let's kiss this time."

"I'm sorry," I say, looking down. "I'm sorry for everything. I...God, I've felt so uneasy lately. But whatever's wrong with me, I don't want you to be unhappy. I only want you to feel happy."

"You love witches," she says with a shrug. Then she closes her eyes and gently lifts my chin, kissing my lips. "You love *us*. The mystery. The—" She closes her eyes and kisses my lips gently again. "Occult secrets. *Alondra*. Her beguiling ways. *Arcana*. Her secretiveness. Her...*evil*."

"I hate your evil."

"Hate me then." But then she kisses my lips again. "Fight me. Hurt me. Love me. And then, Liam Johansen, handsome husband of mine. Fuck me."

I laugh. But she looks so sincere, nodding and gazing deeply into my eyes.

She stands up and removes her robe, revealing a dark blouse and slacks, and lays it on a chair. I think she was wearing the same blouse and slacks two years ago. Then, standing over me, she slowly unbuttons her blouse.

"I don't want you to be sad," I mutter.

"Show me."

Then she removes her bra. In the flickering candlelight, I gaze upon her pale breasts and nipples. Then she pulls down her pants. She lays both the pants and the shirt on the chair. And then, in just thin white panties, she straddles my lap. She runs her hand along my cheek and beard. And I smell her. God, I think it's the same wonderful smell of vanilla and sage she wore back then.

"Now, I guess I'm breaking tradition," she says with a chuckle, kissing my lips. She grips my legs more tightly with hers while rubbing her tongue along mine. "I don't remember sitting on you. I guess that's new." Then she whispers, "Come on, babe. Let's make a baby. Let's do it on our two-year anniversary. Not our wedding anniversary. The anniversary of the first day I met adorable, fiery you. You don't want me to be sad? Then let me tell you a little secret. The first day of my life, Liam, when I didn't feel sad was when I first met you. I never really found happiness after Mom and Dad died. Not even with Jane. I wasn't happy until I met you."

I rub my fingers along the soft skin of her stomach, over her belly button. She lifts my shirt. I lift up my arms to help her. Then she runs her hands along the short hairs of my chest and over my abs. And then, coming close and pressing chest to chest, lips to lips, we kiss again in all that flickering candlelight.

"Liam, you didn't cheat on me," she whispers. "When I was sick, I watched you from the bedroom. You don't have it in your heart to cheat. But, my naughty boy, you did make out a lot with Silvia. You both disrobed, she was naked, and if you had wanted to make love to her, she would have definitely made love to you that night." She touches my lips with hers—hard, as if wanting to hurt me. "I must admit... I enjoyed watching you squirm a minute ago when I made you think you had sex with her."

"Bitch."

She nods, pressing her lips hard over mine again.

"And you love that," she whispers, unclasping my belt and pulling my pants and underwear down to the floor. She runs her fingers along my cock, rubbing it up and down slowly. I pull her closer, stroking her back as she continues to pleasure me. Then my fingers run over her panties. I yank them down her legs. Then I touch between her legs, fingering inside her pussy gently while still touching my lips to hers.

"I'm *your* bitch," she whispers. "And you want to fuck that, don't you? So why don't you? This wicked witch wants you to make love to her tonight. Don't you want to do that, Liam? Don't you want to fuck me?"

Yes. So I throw her off me.

She gasps, landing on her feet. Then she laughs at the violence. She stands up straighter, presenting the whole amazing profile of her naked body, the curves of her breasts and ass, but with her gaze now directed through the window toward the dark woods. Candlelight flickers over her naked figure. And I smell vanilla and sage again. Then she gazes hungrily at me over her shoulder.

I jump up.

Then I shove her toward a small section of the wall between the window and our dining room cabinet. The cabinet full of china shakes. I grab her and spin her around. Her eyes are wide with excitement. So I lift her whole body up in my arms, pushing her against the wall. She laughs and nods. My roughness seems to only excite her more. Then, as I embrace her tightly, lifting her up high, my cock enters her.

Everything is happening so fast. But her willingness, how thrilled she is, her daringness move me. I feel like if I do exactly what she wants and fuck her right here and now, I can finally make her happy. It's what she wants me to do.

And so that's what I'm doing. I'm pushing in and out, feeling the pleasure grow. I'm also more vocal than before, finding myself moaning as loudly as she does. Usually, I'm quiet, and she seems to respond more fervently to that too.

I'm squeezing the soft skin on her ass, as I lift her whole body up and down. Her weight is taxing and painful in my arms, but she's moaning louder between every laugh. And that's arousing me even more.

But best of all, with all our tension and sadness lately, she's smiling. That means everything to me. I haven't seen a smile, a genuine smile like this, on her face for so long.

But she clambers out of my embrace and turns her back to me.

"Do me from behind," she says, gazing over her shoulder. She gestures to the wall. "Do it." Her lips curl. "Fuck me. Yes, like an animal. Screw me from behind. Don't you want to fuck your witch, warlock? Devour me. Love me. Break me. Tear me apart. Destroy me. Fuck me."

I answer by throwing her body against the wall again. She catches herself with her palms, laughing harder than ever. Then I stroke the soft skin of her back, all the way down to the curve of her ass. As I run my fingers along the crack, squeezing her butt tightly, she moans. My hands roam back up toward her chest and along the curves of her breasts. Her nipples are hard.

Our lips touch again as she looks back.

"Oh, God, I love you so much," she says, almost pained, with her head leaning back. I kiss her lips, playing with her tongue again. "I love you."

I enter her again.

The forest in our side yard is full of a white mist reflecting the moonlight. A tinge of red emanates from the faraway tree trunks. Strange. The scarlet seems to be mixing with the white, creating an almost pink mist along the ground. And that red mist seems to be pushing toward the window, creeping slowly, like a fog, toward our house. It's red, like the red of the Abaddon coven. But now it's also mixing with the yellow of the candles, flaming like elemental fire. It reminds me of the red I once saw in our bedroom. But then it was Melanie's conjuring. This is our magic spell. No...this is *my* magic spell.

I desire her so fucking much now. I have this burning desire to be one with her. To take my wife and push her so hard, all the way through the wall, that both of us are torn asunder, only to join and become one. Press into her. Break her. Break me. Because...maybe this is the only way we can finally conceive a child? I want so much for her to have my baby. Not for me, but for her happiness. Cadence. Our daughter. Alondra's been so sad, so depressed. Maybe if she could become pregnant with this girl, our daughter, all of our problems would fade away? Maybe my wife could be happy again? Happy like she was when I first met her in this house?

"That's it, babe," she coaxes. "Deeper. Yes. Make us have that daughter you saw in your vision. You saw her, right? Let's...yes, let's make that happen tonight. Make her tonight!"

The red light seeps through the windows and walls, filling the entire room with red and yellow smoke. Then flames form along the walls. That's strange. Fire seems to ignite at the base of every wall in the room, as if gasoline had been poured on the foundations of our dining room. And the red smoke becomes so thick, like a thick, intoxicating brew of smoke and flame, enveloping both of us. It doesn't make me cough. It doesn't make me fear that we'll burn. I feel like it's simply a vision of our passion. It's just a burning flame, as hot as our mutual desire.

The walls disappear.

We're outside now, on the wild grass of our side yard, in Hawthorne Forest. And Alondra's no longer leaning against a wall—her breasts and stomach are rubbing against the thick spiky bark of a tree trunk. She's panting and moaning. And I'm pressing into her, harder and harder, over and over, from behind, cushioned by her ass while caressing her tits. Her moans have become more like screams now.

"That's it, babe!" she says. "Fuck me. Let's make a baby!"

Tears flow from my eyes. I don't know why. All this passion is not getting rid of the terrible things that won't leave my head. I feel sad. And I think all of this isn't for my pleasure—it's simply so she doesn't feel the same dread.

The red blurs.

So I press harder. Faster. And I groan. All the while, I squeeze her soft breasts and erect nipples. Despite all my despair, I still feel carnal desire, touching her soft skin. It's such a tangled, fucked-up mix of emotions. On one hand, every thrust disguises sorrow. On the other hand, I can't wait for the next punch. The next hit. Screwing her cannot stop the tears that pool in my eyes, no matter how much we hurt. I feel sick. And yet I want to live in this crazed moment forever and ever. I think I could. I think I could burn in hell if it meant experiencing such pleasure.

Is this hell? An eternity of pleasure amid absolute dread, fear, and rage? Torture? A desire never quenched?

"Fuck you!"

My voice sounds alien, deeper than usual.

"Yes!" she says. *"Yes!* Fuck me! Oh, do it. Fuck me hard. I love you so much! Let's make a baby!"

Stop!

"That's it. That's it, Lee. Don't stop now."

Stop it!

"Yes! I love you. I love you so much!"

Stop!

I lurch back, and the room reappears. I stumble. I grope along the window. I feel so dizzy and sick. My forehead hits the glass. And then I just stare outside at the dark trees lit in moonlight.

I feel tears flowing down my face. I try so hard to

suppress a whimper and hide my face from her. I can't let her see me crying. That would ruin everything. All I wanted tonight was for my wife to be happy.

I'm so scared.

Then I jump as I feel someone grope me from behind, kissing my neck and back while running a hand through my hair. But the most awful thing is, I want to escape. Alondra was right. She always seems to be right. I want to run outside into the woods and leave her tonight. I want to get out of this house and never come back. I want to do exactly what she feared I'd do two years ago. Exactly what she feared I'd do now. And the nausea, all my hatred, will go, if I just go.

But she won't let me. She's grasping me so tight.

Slowly, she turns me around and presses her whole naked body into mine, her breasts pressed against my chest. She's groping for me, kissing me, and squeezing me. Then she digs her head into my chest.

"Don't," she whispers, clutching me in an embrace against the cold glass behind me. Her voice cracks. *Is she crying too?* She kisses my bare chest and shoulder. "Don't go. Don't ever do that."

Her breasts press against my chest again, arousing me again. I try to pull away, but I can't. I really don't want to. I want to be in her embrace forever. Even if it's my last breath, taking me down into the very pits of hell again. Residing in the depths. I think I could do that for an eternity.

I'm sure now she sees my tears. But she doesn't say anything. She just buries her head in my shoulder. To hide her tears too?

I surrender as she presses me harder against the large glass window. I surrender...everything.

"I've...foreseen, baby," she mutters, sounding almost desperate. "That one day you will leave me."

"I'm sorry, Alondra. I'm so sorry for everything bad that's happened to us."

I feel more tears flow from my eyes, even falling on her hair. She nods, digging her head into my chest.

All is quiet. Dark. All that redness is gone. And all those candles, still lit, strangely seem dimmer than before.

But my wife remains in my arms.

"Did you like our dinner?" she finally asks, almost deadpan.

"Yes."

"Do you love me, Lee?"

"Yes, I do."

"I love you, forever and ever."

"Yes, Alondra. I will love you forever too."

I hate this world.

11

CAGES

I'M LISTENING TO GENTLE PIANO MUSIC BLARE THROUGH THE speakers of my car while driving across the state line into Florida. The state line is only about an hour and a half from our forest town, closer than heading up north to Atlanta. It's just that the next city, Jacksonville, is still another hour west after crossing from interstate seventy-five to ten. I really didn't intend to leave Georgia. I just wanted to leave our tall trees for a change in scenery. Then, after two hours, I found myself driving some more. I suppose I had to get away.

I'm listening to the song "Tonight." Alondra's right. This new double CD, "Mellon Collie and the Infinite Sadness" by the Smashing Pumpkins is better than "Siamese Dream," the album she gave me when we first met. It just is. I mean they're both amazing. Maybe this new album is better because, as a double album, "Mellon Collie" has so many tracks? Here comes "Jellybelly." *Fuck yeah!* Alondra and I really should see them live in concert. That distortion and heavy rock is pure perfection. It really is. I really have no idea what the hell Billy Corgan's saying, but it doesn't matter. You know what I mean? I mean, it's just a fucking great song.

And there I go pressing harder on the gas pedal.

It always seems brighter in Florida. It's like the sun decides to finally creep out of the clouds, looking onto the earth, and shine two times brighter here than anywhere else in the country. With all those trees turning a brighter green on both sides of this four-lane highway, it's like I am finally really seeing light for the first time.

And there go three motorcyclists racing past me. The energy seems to turn up whenever I travel down to Florida.

Maybe Alondra and I should move here?

What am I saying? She's never going to move out of Hawthorne. She's got a Southern Belle witch castle in the woods that totally fits her. Even Hawthorne Forest fits her. I mean Hawthorne *is* Alondra.

There's a large turtle on the shoulder of the freeway. That's pretty cool.

Hey, now...what song is this? I don't know. I mean, Allie and I have heard the album now a million times, but we don't really know the names of most of the songs. We love this new album. I've got the other CD on the passenger seat, and I really have no idea where I put the sleeve. I think I lost it in her house. Whatever the song is, it's amazing.

I had to get away. I didn't even tell Allie. But Alondra doesn't care when I disappear. You know, if we ever do have a daughter, I think her mom's gonna let her do whatever the hell she wants.

Beneath it all...I feel worried. Nervous. Unsettled. And nothing any of my friends can tell me will take that away. Tomorrow's the first day of school. And there's that too. Alondra's gonna be working on her dissertation with Dr. Kriegel, and I'm going to be a junior in psychology. Just another year at Hawthorne—as long as there are no possessed children popping up in class or ghosts haunting the student halls this time.

I change the song track.

Ah, here's probably the most popular song on the album, which is always on the radio: "Bullet with Butterfly Wings." What an irony. The first line talks about vampires. Coincidence? Jungian synchronicity? My friend Billy would call it synchronicity. Then again the lead singer, *Billy* Corgan, isn't talking about witches—he's talking about vampires. But witches and vampires are kinda the same thing, aren't they? They're both gothic.

Coincidences really creep me out. Allie and I have talked about that a million times before. So many things seem to pop up seemingly spontaneously that give meaning to our lives if we pay enough attention to them. Words like *Billy*, *vampires*, and *cages* seem really fitting right now.

I think it's time to head home.

12

———

SNACKERS

I'm sitting in a white vinyl booth across from Billy in a small café called Snackers. It's only a block away from Hawthorne University. With its windowed walls, booths, and stools at a long counter, it was probably originally a coffee shop. Now the place has been transformed into, quite possibly, the most popular hangout at Hawthorne University on this Saturday night. Especially this week, when classes are just starting.

I stare out at the darkness through a large window to my left. I'm already buzzed. There's a one-lane road, and beyond the road are trees. Lots of trees.

Bill's such a nerd that he grabbed our table the minute the people sitting in it left. Now everyone's looking down on the two of us for sitting in a booth big enough to seat four. A couple of times, a drunken student just sat on the edge of our booth. I don't mind. Bill and I can be pretty shy when it comes to confrontation, you know. But if Alondra were here, she'd probably say something. No...actually, if Allie were here, she would have stopped Bill from reserving this table.

It smells like pizza and burgers. Those smells are mixed

with occasional whiffs of perfume and cologne from all the student bodies.

Every weekend Snackers is a fire marshal's nightmare. Most students are just standing. A great many others are in line near a counter. All the while, behind the counter, four workers dressed in white are moving chaotically in and out of the kitchen, handing plates of food to people standing in a long line.

"Look, what I'm trying to say," Bill says with a slur, slinging a glass mug around, "is that cider was a total favorite of the founding fathers here in America. John Adams had it every goddamn fuckin' morning. Can you believe that? For breakfast. They all drank alcohol like fishes gulping up water, three times more than we drink, I tell you. I should know, I study history. Not as much colonial history as your wife, but I study. I study. Cider's something people don't think about a lot today. They really didn't drink much beer back then. I can see why. I tell you, apple cider is absolutely fucking great. Like this. Hey...where the hell's your wife anyway?"

"She has some catching up to do with Dr. Kriegel."

"Oh, well..." He drinks more cider. "Drink up, Lee, and enjoy it before we're back to work. Hey, are we getting those cheese sticks? Those were awesome, man."

"I don't know," I say with a chuckle. "I'm not sure I really want to brave the crowds right now, Billy."

"Excuse me," slurs a girl in a white T-shirt and jeans, laughing. She just sits down beside me at the edge of the booth. Then she scoots further into the seat, stealing more real estate.

"We probably should stand," I suggest.

"Fuck them," Bill drawls. "Hey, maybe let's...let's get some food, Lee. Anyway, you got cider during the Constitution. You got cider right around the Bill of Rights and, probably, right around that Boston Tea Party. I tell you, they could have thrown that shit in the water, instead of tea. The founding fathers drank the stuff all the time. So try some. It's better than beer, I tell you. It's my new thing, you know.

"Colonists also had lots of hard liquor, of course, like... whiskey. You know, moonshine. Porter beer was big too. And wine. Sure, of course, lots of wine was everywhere. I mean, where is there ever not wine? Or mead, that ancient sweet honey wine that's been around since Thoth and those Egyptians. Actually...did they have wine? How should I know? But cider, cider must have been there, man. And cider is the best drink in the whole goddamn world."

"Hi," says the girl, turning to me with a smile. "Hey, you don't mind me sitting here with my friend, do you?"

I shrug and drink more beer from my mug. Then Bill stares blankly out the window.

"Why don't I get those cheese sticks?" I suggest to Billy, getting up.

"They were out last time, man. But, hey, if they don't have that shit, grab some potato skins, would you? Those were great too. Anything fried or salty. And hey, Liam, can you get me another drink?"

"Cider or beer?"

"Who fucking cares," he drawls.

I get up—or try to. I have to wait for the girl by my side to stop yapping to her friend and give me enough space to brave the aisle. Then, slowly, I make my way through the ton of packed bodies. Glancing back for a second, I see that I'll be standing when I get back. The inebriated girl and her friend are now sitting across from Bill. Bill doesn't mind. He's striking up a conversation—probably about apple cider.

Everyone is moving. And I don't mean walking—I mean everybody is swaying as if I'm unsteady in a boat, shifting up and down, side to side, like waves on the sea. I'll be regretting all these beers tomorrow.

And now I find myself standing by the counter with twenty others, sipping my beer and waiting for potato skins.

Or did I order cheese sticks? Ha, I don't even know.

A lady from behind the counter hands the person in front of me a plate. Then she hands me a cider mug and a plate of skins.

I make my way, shoulder to shoulder, back to the booth, lay the plate by Bill, and hand him another mug. Then I stand uncomfortably over the two girls.

They laugh and get up.

"Just let me scoot by the window," I say to the girls. "You two can sit here if you want. There's room."

But the strangers flash a grimace at Bill, laugh, and shake their heads.

"Got you potato skins and cider, Bill."

"You're the man. Cider's so much better than beer, you know. Did I tell you about the founding fathers?"

And then we just sit and people watch. Which I don't mind. Of course, Bill ogles women. I stare at a Falcon's game on a large mounted TV.

~

"Abaddon. Abaddon. Abaddon."

What the hell?

The lights turn off.

It gets dark.

You'd think with the place packed, I'd hear shouts and gasps with all the lights turned off. But I hear nothing.

Then I lurch back. Because Billy's no longer sitting across from me. In the darkness, replacing him, is this older woman covered in filth and mud, naked and bare-breasted, with long, really thin hair. Her eyes are bright white and seem to shine amid all the mud on her face. She's so filthy that every slight turn stains the peach booth black. Wait... peach? I thought the booths were white?

Swinging around, I gaze at an empty restaurant. It's so dark. And all the students standing over me have disappeared. The whole place has been transformed, lit now only by the white moonlight outside. White snow is piled under a street lamp. Large peppermint sticks and reindeer decals are affixed to walls, and strings of red and green lights hang from the ceiling. And everything smells...of creamy chocolate. That's when I notice that the wooden tabletop is coated in a dark, melting goo.

The monster's cracked and gray lips curl into a grin.

"I told you before, Cadence," the woman says. *Her voice is Melanie's!* But her features are older, reminding me more of her mom. "People cry and cry and cry. And like I said before, if you throw too much ice cream on the table—" She gestures at all that chocolate ice cream. "What do you get? A big fucking mess, if you ask me. I told you and Maddie back home that I don't like witches, and I sure don't like ice cream. I don't want to come down and cast magic again. Yule's been here ever since I learned witchcraft, but she could never tempt me or Alondra. Because while Samhain sure loved her magic, Alondra and Liam were sure in love with themselves."

"*Get out!*" I shout, hammering the table, making some of the ice cream splatter. "*Get the hell out of here! Vade retro! Vade retro! Go away!*"

"Go home now, Liam," Melanie says, opening her eyes wide. "Go home! Your wife is sick."

She disappears.

I squint as lights flash back on brightly. All the bodies surrounding our booth have returned. That same football game is on the TV. The booths are back to white, and there are no more ice cream or Yuletide decorations. But now everyone standing over us is staring down at me.

"Are you okay, man?" Bill asks, leaning forward. My drunk friend looks so surprised that he seems sober.

No, I'm really not.

I jump up. But then I swoon, nearly falling right back down on the booth.

"I...I gotta go, Bill. Shit, I had way too much...to drink. I'm gonna...just walk home. I'm gonna go."

"Sure. Sure, man. Of course, neither of us will be driving tonight. But you said *vade retro*. Did you mean that? Did you see something? Why were you shouting an incantation, man?"

"Never mind. I...I thought you were Melanie—or her mom or something. Whoever appeared said Alondra is sick back at the house. I have to go back home and check on her."

"That devil kid was here?" he asks with his eyes wide.

"More like her older self."

"Sounds like a trap, dude. Let's go." But he can barely get up.

"No, stay here. That freak has popped up before. If every-thing's okay, I'll come right back. It's early enough."

"Sounds fucking creepy, man. All right, let me...let me know then. Shit." He rubs his eyes and shakes his head. "We're having fun, right?"

I try to unlock and open our front door quietly.

She's probably in bed.

When I open the door, Sheba, our black cat, scurries like a shadow down the hallway toward the guest room to my left. Then I look up the stairway toward the second floor—it's dark. It's dark down the hallway toward the dining room and living room too.

I'm wobbly. The ground is still moving. And my head's starting to ache. That means I'm at the plateau of my buzz. Well, it's downhill from here.

About halfway up the stairs I notice a faint light emanating from the bedroom above. It could just be moonlight coming in through the window, if the drapes are open. I go up the stairs and turn a corner, and I stumble into our bedroom.

Alondra's lying on her back on the carpet with the light from our bathroom shining over her. She's in her black nightgown. It looks like she tripped on her way to bed. Her head is facing to the side and one of her eyes is weirdly half-open.

But that's hardly it. Leaning over her, touching her chest, is a translucent girl in a black robe with a hood over her head. Melanie.

Melanie looks up. Like cat eyes, her eyes flicker white.

"You should probably let her die," she whispers. "She's had too much chocolate ice cream and sweet wine, I think."

"My God, what have you done!"

"Friends told me she was sick," the kid says with a shrug. "I told you to come and help her. Cadence and I are just trying to help you."

"Allie! Allie!"

I fall beside her. I don't care about the little demon. I shake Allie's shoulders. I touch her cheeks. Her eyes close. She's completely limp in my hands... God, it reminds me of Melanie's dead father!

"Alondra! Wake up! Wake up!"

"She just doesn't seem to be moving," Melanie says, now

standing over us. "But...I kind of think Hawthorne would have been a whole lot better if she just died."

"Get out of here!"

And she does. The kid vanishes.

"Allie! Allie! Please. Please! Alondra, wake up."

Alondra's eyes blink. Then she growls this bizarre sound, closing her eyes tightly.

I shake her again.

She doesn't open her eyes.

"Alondra! Alondra!"

I squeeze her fingers. Her hand is limp. So I shake her again.

Then I rush out of the room.

My wife, being the stubborn nature-witch she is, insists on having only one television and two telephones in our house. The phone upstairs in the study isn't connected. So now I'm leaping, or stumbling—I'm so fucking drunk—through more of the darkness. I make my way along the wall until I reach our phone in the kitchen.

I call 911.

Then I'm right back to rushing in the darkness, quickly making my way down the hallway to our guest room. I grab my book, *Broomstick*, hidden in the bottom drawer of the cabinet.

And then I'm running back upstairs, leaping two steps at a time.

I rush to the bedroom and sit by Allie's side again. Laying one hand on Alondra and the other on my book and focusing all my intent, I...I try to calm myself.

Shit. Calm! Really? How the hell am I going to do that?

I take in a deep breath. Breathe in and out more slowly, focusing only on her. I use every breath to try to still my mind. I slow every thought... Alondra taught me how to center myself in meditation. She's told me over and over that, through focus, our magic sharpens.

"*Cura. Cura. Cura.* Alondra. Come on. Come on, Allie. Wake up. Alondra. God. *Cura. Cura. Cura!* Open your eyes. Come on." My hope is that maybe, just maybe, if witchcraft hurt her, my witchcraft can save her. "*Cura. Cura. Cura! Be well again.*"

Her eyes don't open.

Alondra once told me the book held enough power to heal the sick. Well... not by my hands.

13

HAWTHORNE HOSPITAL

I'M IN A LOUNGE CHAIR ACROSS FROM THE HOSPITAL BED IN A small drab, ugly room with whitewashed walls. There's that artificial alcohol smell that I hate. And I'm just staring at Allie. She still hasn't opened her eyes. Behind me is a large window overlooking the hospital parking lot and Hawthorne Forest. It's dark due to heavy cloud cover, and the dim yellow light from the hospital hallway shines over Allie's bed. A few plastic wires are taped to my wife's arm, which connect to a machine on a metal hanger. There's also a red plastic bag full of blood. She won't awaken. But occasionally she winces, and she's squeezed my hand a few times. But her eyes won't open. The nurse says she's not in a coma, thank God. But her newest problem, aside from pain, since the emergency room, has been difficulty breathing. She keeps struggling to breathe. Christ...she's just so, so, sick.

My headache rages, with pressure crushing both sides of my head—probably from the goddamn hangover. I drank wanting to feel good. Now I'd do anything to be sober.

Yellow light from the outside hallway floods the room.

Then a man in a long white coat, his hair peppered with gray, enters the room. I think the nursing staff hates me now. I kept demanding to see her doctor. But the emergency room doctor wouldn't tell me anything. And then, of course, this older guy—the doctor?— completely ignores me as he walks to Alondra's side, glancing up at the machine and all those plastic wires on a metal rack by her bed.

"I'm looking for the doctor."

"I'm Doctor Coleman," says the man. But he's not smiling. He's studying the damn machine. Then he leans down and looks at a bag under the bed.

I jump up, moving too quickly. That makes me swoon.

"How is she, doc? Will...she be all right?"

He takes out his stethoscope, puts the thing in his ears, and places the end against her chest. Then he just listens. He shakes his head. That, of course, freaks me out.

"How is she? I'm her husband, Liam."

"You're her husband?" he asks, looking up, amused. "Was she drinking last night?"

"No."

"Hmm. I thought I smelled alcohol in the room."

"What the hell's wrong with her? I found her in our bedroom unconscious. I think she was getting ready for bed, because the light was on by her vanity mirror in the bathroom. But she was unresponsive. So—"

"I read the chart."

"What's happening to her? Why is she out of breath? That started when the ambulance took her to the emergency room."

He folds his stethoscope and drops it into the pocket of his white coat.

"Your wife is out of breath because there's not enough blood perfusing her lungs. Her heart is suffering because of her loss of blood. She is severely anemic. That's why she passed out at home, and that's why she's unresponsive and struggling to breathe. We're giving her transfusions."

"The heart? Then why is she struggling to breathe?"

"Has she fallen unconscious like this before?"

"No."

"I've reached out to Obstetrics. You told the ER physician she had a miscarriage a few weeks ago. Did she see a doctor after the miscarriage?"

"No."

He nods, lifting an eyebrow.

"Will she be all right?"

"We'll have to wait and see," he says with a sigh. Then he rubs his eyes. "She's lost a lot of blood. Her hemoglobin was ranging around five when she was admitted. We'll keep you posted."

"Are you her doctor?"

But he heads to the door, not answering me.

"Wait," I say. "Wait. Wait a minute. Why does she keep clutching at her chest? She's moaning. Is her heart hurting? And she keeps gasping for air. Is there something wrong with her heart? Did she have a heart attack?"

I'm picturing Melanie crouched over her. Lucius died of a heart attack.

"Her heart was damaged by the lack of blood," he answers with a nod.

"So what are you going to do about her heart? Her breathing? And how long do you think—"

"This is all going to take time, sir," he interjects, holding the door ajar. "I won't know how your wife is going to fare until later in the afternoon, or even perhaps tomorrow. But now that she's in our care, we're giving her blood and watching her. It's all about getting blood back into her body. The blood helps her breathe and nourishes her heart. That's all. It's up to her how she's gonna heal. Let her rest. And...

why don't you get some rest?" He sighs. "Why don't we all get rest. It's only four o'clock in the morning."

Then he shuts the door.

I'm left alone in the dark.

I stand over Alondra. Her chest rises and falls gently now. At least she's not groaning anymore or clutching her chest. She appears to just be sleeping. But there's no way I'm going to be resting.

Melanie was leaning over her, touching her chest, when I entered the room. Just like she did when she attacked Lucius. Did that little piece of shit hurt her? Of course she did. Lucius passed away of a heart attack, Silvia told me. His heart was damaged, just like Alondra's now. And Allie said that he was vulnerable because he was alone. Well, with school just starting, and not all our witches in town yet, Alondra was alone too. Her coven still hadn't met for their first ceremony. She was alone and vulnerable, just like Lucius. And now her heart is damaged? Right?

Oh my God.

I stand by the hospital window. Outside the sun is rising, but it's misty and dark under all that cloud cover. It's still drizzling and water is dripping on the glass and collecting in puddles in the cement parking lot below. From this height on the second floor, I can see a valley of shadowed trees for miles. I can imagine if the trees weren't there, to my right, I'd see our college. Almost straight below would be our house.

Then it starts to pour. It's like a white wall of water covering the glass. I catch a red-and-blue glow as an ambulance drives onto the street to my left. I hear its sirens. The red and blue flash through the mist.

Down in the darkness, I see a woman holding a hood over her head, crouched down, carefully avoiding puddles as she walks past drenched parked cars. Her back is turned and it's tough to make her face out. It almost seems like she's wearing one of our black robes. Then I see a smaller person, in a similar cloak, rush past her through the empty parking lot wheeling a small cart. The girl seems to be pushing something wooden in the pouring rain. It almost appears to be a small coffin...or...

There's children's laughter.

"Is she getting better, Mr. Johansen?" asks Melanie's voice from behind. I whirl around but there's nobody there. "I sure hope she does."

"Liam," Alondra mutters in bed. "Liam." Her eyes are shut. "Oh, Lee, please..."

"What, Allie?" I ask, rushing back to the bedside. "What? What is it? What can I do to help you?"

But she's gone back to sleep.

I turn back to the window. But the room brightens in light from the hallway before I can see what the hell that vision was outside.

Two women wearing thick black gothic makeup enter the room. I recognize eyebrow-less and short-haired Cline in suspenders, a white T-shirt, and tight black slacks. But it takes me longer to recognize the golden-haired woman in a loose gray T-shirt and jeans as Silvia. Because usually my friend Silvia is smiling. Silvia looks as down and seems as upset as Cline.

"Hi, Liam," Silvia says gravely.

"High Priest," says Cline with a nod. She stands over Alondra. "I see filth has assaulted her newest victim. The leader of your coven."

"We came as quick as we could, Lee," Silvia says with a frown. "Did the doctors say she's going to be all right?"

"How did you know?"

"Androgyne here felt that Falconsong was sick."

"I can barely get any information from them," I say. "They just say she's anemic."

"Execrated," Cline says, shaking her head. "She's been execrated, Liam. And it is all due to the wicked witch. Doctors can't do anything when mud curses magi. Only we can fight her curses."

Cline takes out a silver cross and pentacle from her purse. She lays the pentacle on Alondra's stomach and the cross on her chest.

"It's time to take care of her once and for all," Cline says.

"We felt like something like this was going to happen," Silvia says. "This is what we were all waiting for here in Hawthorne. Well, now we're here to help."

"We need your book," Cline says, still staring at Allie. "As you know, this monster is powerful. She's warded off our curses, shielding herself behind your coven's magic. Her shield spells are based on your witchcraft. Our curses are potent enough—" She takes out a lipstick tube. Then she brushes the black lipstick over Allie's forehead, forming a triangle. "But we are in need of your magic. We need to fight witch against witch. We need your Book of Shadows and grimoire against the witch's conjuring. It is Kurt's and my belief, Liam, that you can hurt this kid. And we are going to help you do it." She brushes another backward triangle on top of the first. "Silvia said she saw mud residing at the house in Geneva Forest."

"What the hell are you doing?" I ask. These ladies are so used to their spellcasting that I'm not even sure Cline realizes it looks weird to me.

"Sigils enhance the aura around your wife," Cline explains.

She pulls out a metal hexagram on a thin silver chain—a unicursal hexagram necklace, one of Aleister Crowley's sigils. She turns to Silvia. Silvia nods and lifts Allie's head. Then Cline puts the necklace over Allie's neck.

"Hail Satan," Silvia mutters.

"Hail Satan," echoes Cline.

"There's great power in these symbols, warlock," Cline says. "Your wife knows that. Let us help her. Doctors may poke and bleed her body, but we can heal her soul with the help of our energies."

"Let our god help you," Silvia says with a nod, forcing a smile. "It'll be okay. Androgyne is so amazingly powerful, Liam."

Cline looks upon her work on Allie's body and nods in satisfaction. I'm not so sure Dr. Coleman is going to approve when he returns.

"Please, leave this on her after we leave, okay?" Silvia asks me. "All these things will help Falconsong recover."

"You can be the instrument that helps our order stop the little bitch," Cline says with a smile. "Don't think that mud is so naive and innocent. There are thoughts inside that little head of hers. The kid must be punished. This witch is way too powerful, and too young to control the magic herself. You foiled our previous curse at Alondra's place. I can forgive you, *if* you help stop this beast now—not through exorcism, but by finishing her off. If you finish her, my Abaddon Order will be on your side again. So...though I'm sure this is difficult right now, with all that has happened, the group asks for a decision. Will your magic, unhindered by you this time, join us in fighting the abomination and finally cleanse this mud? If you stop her, all will be well for Alondra and you. If not, I foresee your wife will die."

"Melanie's back home?" I ask.

"Back home in Alabama," Cline replies with a nod. "Yes. Go see her. We can follow you, using your book as a black mirror. Silvia said you were able to cast against her with the grimoire, even on her hallowed ground. That is how powerful Escoba's talisman is. If the girl is harmed through magic, there will be no evidence against you. You're not being asked to visit and shoot her." Cline laughs. "You're being asked to perform magic that will finish her off. Hurt her, and she won't be able to hurt us anymore. If you don't want to kill her, that is acceptable to me and Kurt. As long as you do something to stop her magic. I don't care how you do it. But you must cripple her. Muzzle her. Stop her mind from harming the ether. Abaddon will go with you in spirit. We will be with you every step of the way. *If* you're willing to use your book to finally cleanse mud."

"But I saw a witch in a vision asking me not to hurt her."

"Idiot, do you see this witch under you dying!"

"Cline!" Silvia shouts, frowning. "Fuck! Cline, please, for god's sake, stop it! This is so hard for him."

"Just give me..." I say, falling back in the chair. "Give me some time."

"No," Cline says, shaking her head. "You have no more time. Ask why the child is back at her house. Because that is where you and your stupid witches empowered her. Do you think that her family or local services would allow a girl to return to that fun house in Geneva Forest, Alabama? After everything that happened? After the little bitch killed her own father? Silvia told us the condition of her mom. Do you think that everything would be forgotten and the family would just return to that place and go back to normal?" Cline shakes her head. "This abomination has gone back because that is where her energy is and that is where her demons feed. She is not a girl, Liam. She is a mirror of all the devils residing in that cursed house. She is mud. And we need your help in cleansing her mud. All you did with the book last time you went there was make her possession complete. We're not dealing with a girl anymore, we're fighting larvae-infested filth. These worms are residing in the girl. The worms are her *so-called friends*. She will stay in the house until she has gathered enough negative energy to kill Alondra, your friends, Silvia here, and then finally you. She is using black magic in that house to grow more and more of her power. The longer you wait, the more power she gains. Power for what? Look down right now at your wife!"

"Jesus, Cline!" yells Silvia. *"Shut the hell up! You're being such a bitch! Don't you see, you're hurting him! Lee's my friend!"*

"What do you want me to do to the kid?" I snap with clenched teeth. "I was barely even taught how to perform a spell."

"The book speaks through you, Lee," Silvia says. "It's powerful enough to lead you. Liam, if we don't do something now, that girl is going to go after all of us. The girl is hunting us. I agree with Cline about that. I just don't like how much of a cold fucking bitch Cline is."

Cline grins wickedly and shrugs.

"It almost worked," Cline says. "We already trapped her in your ceremonial fire. Then you turned weak and ended the spell on your hallowed ground. If you don't help us, we won't help you."

Then Cline snatches the pentacle on Allie's belly and the cross. She throws the objects back in her purse. Allie groans, clutching her chest. Coincidence? Magic? I don't know. All I know is it looks like Alondra's suffering again.

"Lee, please," Silvia says, touching my arm. "We can ward off her dark magic with our dark magic."

Alondra groans more.

"Are you doing this!" I shout, pushing Silvia's hand off me. I rush up to Cline. Then I lift up a fist, ready to slug her. I'm so tired. So dizzy. I feel like...I'm about ready to faint. But first, I really want to deck this bitch. But Cline stares at my face deadpan. Then another sick grin grows, and she bursts into laughter.

"Such anger!" Cline says with eyes widening. "Such rage. I adore you, wizard. The doctor was so right about you. I didn't see what he saw in you when I first met you. You hold such fury. You make a magnificent necromancer of the dark arts. Perfect for the power of the book and perfect for Abaddon. Fate has chosen you well, wizard. It chose you to work with us. You can be the one to hurt this girl. It's fitting that you take care of her after everything she's done to your wife."

"The book didn't choose me," I snap. "I kept the book from Allie because she's evil."

And then Allie groans again.

"*Stop it!*" I snap, snatching Cline's arm. *"Just stop it! Leave everything on!"*

"As you wish, wizard," Cline says with another infernal smirk. "But of course."

"You're such a bitch, Cline," Silvia says, shaking her head. "You're so mean. I hate you so much. Just stop it! Liam is my friend, okay?"

"The situation is out of control, Nancy," Cline replies. "And it all stems from this asshole's indecision."

"Just stop hurting her!" I snap, grabbing Cline's arm again.

Cline looks down at my wrist and smiles.

"Liam, our magic only protects Alondra," Silvia says, vehemently shaking her head. "Cline isn't hurting her, she's only removing our protection."

"Then put it back!" I shout. "Put your protection back!"

Cline shrugs. She places the objects back on Allie's body.

"Rest, Falconsong," Cline says, turning to Alondra, patting her hand. "Rest." And, indeed, Allie stops wincing. "Liam, you're the one hurting your wife by not letting us fight this witch. Help us fight our common enemy, and your wife will be well. Will you face mud and cleanse us of all her filth?"

I walk to the window. The pouring rain has turned to a drizzle now. And there's a brighter ray of light off the horizon, brightening the wet parking lot. I recall my vision and shudder. But down in the parking lot, there's no coffin being rolled by a freak-girl.

But I feel someone touch my shoulder.

"Oh, Lee," says Silvia gently, rubbing my back. "Lee, everything's going to be okay. If you just let us help you. We just need the power from your book. If we take care of Melanie, Alondra will get better. Then we'll all be better. You can make us all safe."

"I don't even know how to cast a spell, Silvia."

"Go to the house and the book will guide you, High Wizard," Cline says. "We will be with you. You will not be alone. *If* you act on our mutual enemy. Do it, and do it now, to save your wife."

Silvia kisses my cheek. "Whatever you decide," she says quietly, "I really hope she gets better soon. Okay? Cline's a total bitch, but...she's very, very powerful. She predicts you're going to want to hurt Melanie on your own, so don't worry. I don't think there's any hesitation. I know that when you decide the time is right, you'll help us. Then we can either meet you or be with you in the astral realm to guide and empower you in this fight. Okay?"

I nod.

The view of the parking lot blurs. Because tears are forming in my eyes. But then, just for a moment, I think I see that girl rushing through the wet, dark parking lot rolling a coffin again.

I wake up. I must have drifted off, without knowing it, in the hospital lounge chair. It's still dark, likely still before dawn. I can hear Alondra snoring. That's comforting, in a strange way. I mean, she's not groaning.

Then I squint at a flood of light from the hallway. I think the creak from the hospital door woke me.

"Liam," whispers Rachel. "Hi, Lee. How is she?"

"How is she?" echoes Beth.

That's echoed by a bunch of others entering the room, surrounding her bed. Even my friend Billy's here, but he looks awful. He's behind everyone else, leaning against the doorframe.

"Oh, High Priestess," says Rachel quietly. "High Priestess. Falconsong, what's happened to you. Liam, is she okay?"

"Doctor says she lost a lot of blood, Rache. Sorry I called you guys so late. It's just, everything was so crazy. I'm sure Allie wants you all here now."

"Forget it, Lee," Rachel says, squeezing Allie's hand. "We're all here. Oh, High Priestess. How long do the doctors think she'll have to be here, Liam?"

"The girls were impressed you were able to call for an ambulance at all after all our drinking, bud," Bill quips with a chuckle.

Someone flicks on the main light in the room. And that's horrible. God, all that blinding light is sickening. I wince and shut my eyes tightly. My head feels like it's going to explode. I'm almost sure I hear Bill groan too.

I stumble as I rise from my chair. A few of the girls somehow catch me before I crash onto the hard floor. I stumble into the bathroom, find the toilet, and vomit.

"*Shut off the light, Cindy!*" says Rachel in a forced whisper. "Are you stupid, girl? Lee and Bill were out partying last night."

"Oops, sorry, White Dove. So sorry, Liam."

The lights in the room shut off again.

"What's this thing around her neck?" asks Beth.

"Looks like Crowley stuff," answers Cass.

"It's a hexagram," agrees Rachel.

"That's a unicursal hexagram from Thelema," says Bill.

"Don't take that off!" I shout. I spin around, immediately regretting it, as the whole room seems to tip over. Someone tries to help me up onto my knees by the bathroom door. It's Bill. "Just, don't take that...don't take that off her!"

"Okay," Beth says. "Okay, Lee. Don't worry. We won't."

The whole gang is staring at me. I'm leaning on a wall by the bathroom door feeling so sick.

"It's for her protection," I say. "It's from the Abaddon coven. They came here to help her."

"We won't take it off, Lee," Rachel says. "Sure. Don't worry. God, Bill, how much did you guys drink last night?"

"I lost count," he mutters sickly.

Then Alondra says something incomprehensible. That's enough for everyone in the coven to crowd around her again.

"High Priestess? High Priestess?"

Everyone's shaking her and trying to get her attention.

"Knock it off, guys," Rachel says. "Stop it. Let her rest."

"But why isn't she opening her eyes, White Dove?" asks Cindy.

"She still won't open her eyes," Rachel says, choking up.

"I think she's execrated," Beth says, fighting back tears too. "Don't you think, Liam?"

"Any word from the doctor?" asks Rachel.

"The doctor died," replies Mom. "He left us after the girl attacked him in his backyard, making his heart stop. Just like Melanie attacked my daughter-in-law. That's what the Abaddon Order claims. Ain't that right, Liam? Isn't that what you were saying?"

"Liam's not speaking anymore, Mom," says Alondra. "He

hasn't said a word all day. He just keeps staring. I think it's because I won't wake up."

"Stubborn girl."

"Bairn. Bairn, Maverick. Bairn. Bairn."

I'm going to hurt you.

"You don't know where to find me," Melanie says with a chuckle.

You're back at your house. I can see you.

"Now why would I go back to my house, Mr. Johansen? That's where all those bad things happened to Ma and Pa. I sure wouldn't want that. Why would I be back there? Think I'm lonely? Think I'm like you? Think I need friends? Don't I have you and all 'em purple-scarlet harlots to entertain me from Hawthorne-land? *Et mulier erat circumdata purpura et coccino et inaurata auro et lapide pretioso et margaritis habens poculum aureum in manu sua plenum abominationum et inmunditia fornicationis eius?"*

"Liam!" shouts Mom. "Liam! What the hell's the matter with him, Uncle Hanley? Why has he been acting like this all day? Why is he just staring at nothing!"

"Execrated."

"It's just so hard for the boy, I reckon," Uncle Hanley says. "So hard."

"He's got this blank stare," Mom says. "What's wrong with him?"

"Execrated."

If Alondra dies, you die.

"I thought you didn't know any magic, warlock?"

If my wife passes away, I'm going to kill you.

"Come and get me."

14

ROAD BLOCK

WE'RE RUSHING BY TREES ALONG A TWO-LANE HIGHWAY. IT'S nearly twilight. This four-hour drive feels like it's lasted for four days. It's taking an eternity to get from Hawthorne to Geneva Forest, Alabama. Maybe it's because it's the first time I've driven here alone? The trees, unlike those at Hawthorne, are scattered, along with quite a bit of marsh-land. Some red and orange fall leaves are showing, but it's mostly green. Under cloud cover and mist, everything feels dark and blurry. Maybe it's because I'm driving too fast? I don't know.

Spiritus. Spiritus. Spiritus.

That's Silvia. See, I'm not alone. It's not just you accompanying me on this trip.

After driving up and down a hilly incline, I rush by a classic red barn with cows grazing by a fence. The color of the barn isn't that far off from the color of my car. To my right, more trees blur. I think I'm near the cemetery I visited with Alondra?

"Everyone kept crying. They kept crying and crying and

crying. It was like Momma. Momma and Winnie could never, ever stop their crying."

Shut up!

"But your wife couldn't cry. She doesn't seem to ever cry. And now, she's too sick to cry."

We'll help you with the girl. Don't worry, Lee. Just get there. Get there now.

I left my friend Billy to watch over Allie. Bill told me to get some rest. Ha. I lied and said I'd head home to Jersey, start a family, and leave Alondra for good. I didn't tell him about this errand. I didn't tell anybody. Except Silvia.

Alondra is sick. Remember that. Spiritus. Compaticus. Completus. Compaticus. That is why we are here with you. But you need to hurry, Liam. Hurry. Androgyne says the girl intends to wander. If she goes on a witch wandering behind her house, her power will grow. Then she'll finish us off and take your crown with us.

Oh, shit! Is that a cop?

Yes, it is! *Fuck!*

The sound of sirens blares amid flashing red-and-blue lights.

So I pull my car over on the shoulder among wild grass and weeds under a thick cover of green leaves. And then I wait as a young officer steps out of a police car. He's a thin guy with a mustache in a black uniform.

I roll down my window.

"Please step out of the car," he says in an Alabama accent.

"I'm in a hurry, officer."

"Well, I can sure see that." He tips down his shades and chuckles. "Did you take a look at your speedometer, mister? While you were barreling through my county? The radar read over a hundred miles an hour. It topped at one hundred and twenty. So, do me a favor and step the hell out of your car."

"I really don't have time for this," I say, shaking my head. But I unbuckle my seat belt.

"Are you high?" he asks.

"Excuse me?"

"Are you high? Are you on drugs? Been drinking? I think I smell alcohol. What the heck do you mean, you don't have time? Step out of your bleeping car. Or, if you're resisting, I'll call for backup and haul you out of there. We're all about law and order in Geneva County."

"But you don't understand," I say. "I have to get to Winona's house. This is an emergency."

"*Get out of the car!* You ain't got no business speeding down my highway like this. Tonight, I'm taking you into the station!"

I reach for the keys in the ignition, shaking my head.

"Leave your keys. You won't be needing them after I impound your car."

I step out.

"Hands over your head. That's it, now. You don't have time... You don't have time." He laughs. "That's a funny one, mister. Tell that to the judge."

I hear the jingle of his metal handcuffs. He grabs my hands and pushes me against the hood. Then he pulls my hands to my back, and I feel the cold metal and hear the click of the cuffs.

Spiritus. Spiritus. Spiritus emphaticum.

Get rid of him now!

That's when, by the shoulder of the road, I see hundreds of dark demons lined up, side by side like sentries, in tattered black robes. It's like an endless black fence lining the shoulder of the highway. Only, under this cloud cover, their white eyes glow in the white mist. They're the Ekimmu

—more Ekimmu demons than I've ever seen, towering at nearly twice the height of any man. But all they do is stand, side by side, perfectly still, lining both sides of the highway for as far as my eyes can see. I'm not afraid of them. No, actually, I feel invigorated by them. And angry. I feel so mad. I feel like pulling the sidearm out of this cop's holster.

The officer notices me looking. Then I realize how insane I must look staring at the side of the road. Surely, he doesn't see these devils?

The demons disappear as fast as they appeared. But I still feel them. Their power is intoxicating. No, *my* power is. These demons empower me.

There's a gust of wind. It's a burst of sudden cold air, making me shiver. The cop seems to notice the cold too, looking about him curiously.

"Curious weather," he says. "Could be a storm." Then he turns back to me. "Wearing those preppy clothes, you don't seem to be the kind of kid who looks for trouble. What the hell were you doing driving so fast? Oh, yeah, you've gotta rush over to somebody's house." He laughs. "I intended on just ticketing you, son, but now you're acting so weird. What are you on? Fess up. Or do I have to test you?"

"I told you," I snap, clenching my teeth, "I just have to get to a little girl's house. I'm not on anything. Yes, I drank alcohol, but that was the other night. My wife's really sick in the hospital."

I just shake my head and heave a sigh.

"Hey, what the hell is this costume you have in your car? Going to a Halloween party already? Halloween is in two weeks, bub."

The officer pulls my black robe from the passenger seat. Inspects it. Then he throws it back on the driver's seat and shakes his head. But that's when he sees *Broomstick*, my hundred-year-old leather-bound Book of Shadows, which was covered by my cloak. And though the coven and I are quite accustomed to my grimoire, the book is old enough to look like it belongs in a museum.

Spiritus. Spiritus. Emphapaticum! Emphapaticum!

Esces. Esces. Esces.

Make him leave. Do it now. Hurry!

"My, what do we have here?" asks the officer with a laugh. "Now that doesn't look like some party prop. Looks like a fancy book, sure does." He walks around the car to the passenger door. "Sure looks old too, mister."

"Don't touch the book."

"Excuse me?" he asks with a laugh.

"I warn you. Do not touch that. Alondra told me long ago that no one can touch that book. You can look at it, just don't touch it."

Esces. Esces. Esces.

"Are you warning *me*, mister? I tell you what. After I take a gander, we're gonna try a sobriety test. And then we'll be heading to the station. Might not be booze, but it's sure something strange you're on. That's for sure."

He shakes his head and laughs again, snatches the book from the passenger seat, and starts thumbing through the pages.

Then he looks bewildered. Of course, my Book of Shadows shows whatever it wants to show the reader. Right now, you're following what's happening to me. That's what the book magically shows *you*. But, for all I know, the book is just showing this officer strange symbols and gibberish. Or it could be completely blank. A book that old showing absolutely nothing would be pretty weird too. Or, the absolute worst possibility: Writing could be appearing in real time as he gazes at it, just like Alondra's handwriting appeared in front of Lucius last year. I don't know. But, of course, like everyone who reads it, he's completely mesmerized.

The "fence" of Ekimmu appears again alongside the highway. This time, I will it. And this time, I summon five of the devils to slowly float over to us. They approach with their tattered black cloths stirring in the wind. Then they surround the police officer.

Though handcuffed, I still have my feet. So I walk around the car and sneak up behind the policeman as he reads. He's still mesmerized by the book.

I tug at my wrists. The metal chains easily break free and clang along the cement road.

Surely, the police officer heard that? But he didn't. He's too fixated on the book.

"*Formido!*" I shout, waving my right palm before him. "*Esces. Esces. Esces. Formido!*"

The police officer looks up from the book. He opens his eyes wide, seeming to finally notice all the demons surrounding him. Then he buries his head in his hands.

"*Somnos! Somnos! Somnos!*"

The officer's body goes limp. He collapses on the asphalt. And all my demons disappear.

There's no time for this, Lee! Get back in your car and find the house. I told you, if she goes out now for a wandering, she'll escape. Then she can cast against me and my friends!

I jump back in the car, turn on the ignition, and quickly make my way back onto the road.

15

───────

BLACK SUN

The road blurs more than ever. On both sides of the two-lane highway, the trees blend into single long streaks. This isn't the first time I've traveled the woodsy road, but somehow things feel so different. Though the sun is out, everything is dark. I mean, everything. Sometimes, I catch the sun peeking out from the clouds. But when it does, it's even weirder, with a bright halo of yellow and a dark center, like a lunar eclipse.

I speed past that narrow, treacherous bridge that marks Melanie's cursed house. Somehow, I make it across alive, slowing down far less than usual to make sure I don't plummet into the water below. Then, after returning to the road, I climb the final incline to her house.

And then... I'm here.

I park my car in front of the house and throw open my door. Everything's changed. Under a sliver of sunlight emanating from the eclipsed sun, dark rays reveal a broken structure, as if the house was damaged by a terrible storm, as if wind and sleet broke the tiles off the roof. The vegetation in the front and side yards has been replaced by mud.

The front door and all the windows are boarded up, with red spray-painted lines on the wooden planks. There's no truck by the shed this time. There are no vehicles at all. The place looks deserted.

"That house is empty," I say aloud to myself.

She's here, Liam. Enter the house. She's hiding and waiting. She senses you. Go into the house before she runs away.

Whispers surround me. Those whispers aren't my friends. I've heard this specter-like murmuring at the house before. Then even now, near twilight, and during a hot day, my body shivers in an unnaturally frigid breeze.

I put on my black robe.

Why am I here?

Your wife is sick. You have to help her.

"Melanie?" I thunder, facing her home. *"Melanie!"*

It starts to rain. This isn't like the last time, when it rained *inside* the house. There's enough cloud cover to believe that this could be a fall storm. Still, the timing—right after I shouted—is alarming.

There's a flash of lightning. Then thunder.

I grab my book and slam my car door shut. Then, before the boarded door, I extend my long black wand.

"*Apertum. Apertum. Ecces. Succutio. Apertum. Melanie! Melanie!*"

The wood planks vibrate. Then the door shakes, as if struggling to open.

"*Apertum! Apertum! Apertum!*"

Wood explodes. I have to shield my face from splinters, and it's enough to bring me down to my knees. When I stand up, the planks on the door have been blown asunder by my mere words. The door creaks open. Inside is complete blackness because of all the boarded-up windows and dark sky. But in the shadows, I recognize familiarity in the freak house.

"Kathy?" I say, entering the house slowly. "Kathy Grant? Winona?"

My words seem loud in the utter silence.

Every piece of furniture in the house is missing. Whereas from before I recall vases and prints of paintings along the walls, every structure has been taken from the home. Last time there were even luggage and clothes by the door. That's gone. But I hear water dripping. Yes, part of the outer demolition must have been from some terrible storm. There's an earthen scent and the muddy carpet slushes under my feet. Slowly, holding my wand in one hand and my book in the other, I enter an even darker hallway. Water drips along these walls too. I can't see it but, touching the wall, I feel moisture. The hallway feels like a cave with most of the light still coming from behind me through the front door I left ajar.

"Melanie!" I shout.

My tennis shoes sink further into soaked wet carpet.

"Melanie? I know you're here. Show yourself."

But why? Why would anyone live in this filthy derelict structure?

I hear crying. It sounds like it's coming from the kitchen.

Passing a familiar stairway, I see the large dining room connecting to the kitchen and living room, still devoid of all furniture. This was where the girl made Agnes fly near the ceiling. And on the other side of the house, near the couch, sat her dead father in a lounge chair. Thank God, the lounge chair and sofa are gone. But now I see the shadow of a kid crying in darkness near the fireplace.

"Melanie?"

"She made us come back," mutters a girl in tears. "She, she said she wanted to play with me here. She was happy when I said yes. She said no grown-ups would disturb our play here anymore. She tried to get Momma to come and play too, but Momma just wouldn't join our games. Mommy refused. Ma's so sick now, Liam. And you already know what she did to Pa."

"Melanie?"

"Winona."

The girl looks up. In shadows, I see the girl's unnaturally bright white eyes. Her skin seems to be coated with as much filth and mud as the stained floor, but it's hard to make out in the darkness. Her body looks thin. I remember her being plump. I suppose no one would be eating much here. Her smell is terrible. It's a rancid mix of urine, feces, and sulfur.

I jump back as the fireplace ignites. Now I see that all the white walls surrounding me are caked in dirt and mud too. And there are large cracks and gashes along the walls, damage that I remember from the first horrible haunting in this demon-house. In the firelight, the floor doesn't look much different from the outdoors—it's covered with rocks and grime. I even see branches and leaves. I can't see outside though. All the large windows are boarded.

This poor little girl blends in with all this dreck. Her body, now in a filthy, shredded dress, is coated in the same black-and-brown sludge as the muddy carpet. *Mud*, as Cline kept calling Melanie.

"She made me come back," Winona adds, brushing long, disheveled, muddy hair from her eyes. "Don't you see? I didn't want to. But she made me. She likes playing with all her friends here. And she still makes me play with her dolls."

"Winona, I came to help—"

"Abaddon, Abaddon," croaks Melanie's voice from another room. "Abaddon. Come to help my family again, sinner?"

Winona's whole body quakes.

"Come to play? Come to play. Play with sister Lucy? Play,

play, play? Cast a spell, cast her away. Sheol? Hell? Graves? Damnation. Don't make no goddamn difference to me."

"*Shut up, Melanie!*" screams a voice from upstairs. That sounds like her mom, Kathy. "*My God, please, won't you please just shut up!*"

"*There be sinners in our house again, Mamma!*" Melanie answers from upstairs. "*Seems they didn't get enough of me last time. Do you feel 'em? Their eyes and ears are everywhere.*"

"I'll take care of him, sister," Winona says, turning back to me. Though her eyes are wet from tears, her muddy face and devilish grin, lit by flickering flames, make me shudder. Then, worse, Winona's white eyes shine brighter.

There's a rattle and slither behind me.

"Where is Melanie, Winona?" I ask.

"*Don't hurt my sister, you bitch!*" Winona cries in a guttural voice. And she growls. "*You're a bad, bad, bad man!*"

Then Winona leaps on me. I'm thrown to my knees, even though the girl weighs practically nothing. I stand with her arms clutching my neck. "*Get off me!*" I try to buck and throw her, but, as she sits on my shoulders those tiny fingers grasp my neck like a vise. I feel her fling her whole body in different directions. But she's laughing. She's acting as if it's all a game. I feel a sharp sting on my neck. God, I think the girl's biting me! And then she starts slashing my face with her hands. I think her dirty fingernails are long enough to cut.

I finally hurl her off me.

There's more laughter in the walls.

"*Stay away from my sister, you bitch!*" screams Winona, jumping on all fours. "*You hear? Stay away, you hear me? Stay away. I warn you! Get the fuck out of my house! This be my hallowed ground, mister!*"

"Is this grown-up botherin' you, Winona?" asks Melanie with a chuckle from another room. "Don't know why he'd come. His mind seems confused. I think he needs us to help exorcise demons from him."

"The warlock says he's come to help us," Winona says. She gazes back at me with those all-white eyes. Blood drips from her mouth—*my blood.* Then she rolls along the wet, muddy floor, bursting into laughter.

"He's helped ewe quite enough, I'd say," Melanie says, laughing too.

Winona leaps up on all fours like an animal. She looks ready to pounce on me again. Then she charges full speed at me, but before hitting me, she turns and rushes straight into the large window. Glass cracks. Outside, wooden boards splinter. But they don't break. She falls back, grinning at me. Then she charges full speed again, throwing her entire body at the window again.

And then again. And then again. And again.

"My God, stop it!" I cry.

I reach for her to stop her violence, but she's moving too fast, hurling herself on all fours, over and over, into the window. Finally, the boarded window bursts from its hinges and is thrown open.

Light brightens up the room as the girl leaps outside. Although it is still dark, the clouds occluding the sun, all that outside light makes me squint.

Winona cocks her head back, on the outside patio, licking her lips, which are dripping my blood over her muddy chin. Shaking her head, she licks the back of her hand. Then she scurries off, vanishing down the grassy hill in the backyard behind the house.

I touch my face. My cheek's wet and there's a sting from a gash.

The power in the house comes from the other one, Liam. Ignore the sister and take care of the true witch.

"Melanie!" I shout, turning back to the house. *"Melanie! Where are you?"*

"Abaddon," Melanie says. "Abaddon. Think I'm hiding from little 'ole ewe? Aw, but you seem confused. Come to help me again? But who, pray tell, is going to help *you*? Seems there be worms squirming around that brain of yours."

"I'm not here to help you! I'm here to make sure you leave me and my wife alone!"

"You came here to make sure I leave you alone? I don't care about your filthy harlot wife. Or her sinner friends. Why would you come all the way here for that?"

She's lying, Liam.

"Kathy," I say looking up. "Kathy, I came back to stop all this. To help you and the kids. Where are you?"

"Momma's gone," Melanie says plainly, walking into the room. The girl's casual and calm manner is unnerving.

She looks and smells as disgusting as her sister. Her face and white dress are caked in mud. And her white eyes seem to shine behind all the muck. Like her sister, she's very thin. And then, like her sister, she runs her hand through her long muddy hair.

"Ma's left us, bully," Melanie says with a shrug. "Cause Winnie and I ran away. But this here be my hallowed ground now, warlock. Remember? And you seem to be in the thick of it. If you came to play, play, play, you best be afraid. Ask Winnie. I never play fair. Especially with grown-ups. But, if you want to know the truth, I'm not sure your mind is here right now. Seems you're not even sure why you're at my house again."

"I need to help my wife."

"I left her alone. Just like I left that leader of sinners alone. I never harmed your wife or that evil man. Just because I came to their side when they were sick, doesn't mean I hurt them. I came to you to tell you that she was sick in Hawthorne, stupid. I told you to get back to the house to go save her. I didn't hurt her. Sinners are busy enough sinning with themselves. Aren't they?"

She's lying, wizard! Stop her now!

I recognize that as Cline's voice this time.

"I will," I say.

"Who, pray tell, are you talking to?" Melanie asks with a grin. Her gray, cracked lips grimace. "Are you talking to the readers of your book? Or is it that order of Abaddon from your Momma's house in Carolina? I don't think adults should want to hurt children. No, I think that's really sick. Especially when their minds aren't all there. Seems adults have enough trouble always hurting themselves."

The girl steps forward. Her hideous appearance, now lit better by the fireplace and the shattered window, make me step back. As does her smell.

"Why are you here?" Melanie asks. Then she frowns. "Aw, do you even know? Poor fella, do you need my sister and I to fix your head? I think—" She looks about the room. "Yes, I think them Abaddon sinners are controlling you. I don't even think you know why."

"I'm...here for my wife!"

"*Liar!*" Melanie shouts, shaking her head. "You came to kill me. Here on my hallowed ground. I might just be a poor little girl, but I read your books of stars. This house here is my hallowed ground. And even with your book, you are helpless under my power. Even if I be just a little girl."

"*Hurt him, sis!*" shouts Winona's voice, with laughter, from outside. "Do it!"

Melanie lifts her chin and sniffs the air. She grows a bigger grin.

"Now hold on, sister," she says, looking around again. "Just you hold on there. Wait, wait, wait just one minute now.

This man didn't come here alone to hurt us. He brought his friends. Not only are they controlling his mind, but they're here. Reckon you're not so dumb after all. You're not alone at all, are you, mister? Ain't I right? You brought a bunch of 'em sinners to hurt us. Should make for quite a game, Winnie." She loses her smile and frowns sadly. "Or, *aw*...do you even know about 'em?"

"Stop playing with him!" cries Winona, popping her head through the broken window. I jump back. Her muddy face is covered with my blood. "Finish him! All he ever wanted was to hurt you and me, Ma and Pa."

"Now let's be patient," Melanie says with a grin, raising a finger. "Be patient, Winnie."

She walks around me, looking behind my back. The girl is looking up, but she doesn't seem to care about me.

"I reckon you're not here alone at all," Melanie says, with a satisfied nod, by my side. "Nope. There's a whole group of 'em red-clothed sinners here. Disgusting men and women in their vestibule watching you. Watching and waiting. Well, well, well, warlock. But while you might bring your friends, I can bring mine. This be my hallowed ground, you motherfucker."

"*Yeah!*" shouts Winona by the window "*Yeah, you tell 'em, sis!*"

"There goes another," Melanie says creepily. "I see you. Come on. Don't be hiding. I saw your shadow pass by the fire of my altar. They're jumpy, Winona. You know why? Because they're scared. You see 'em all shaking now? They're afraid of us."

"Yeah!" Winona cries excitedly. "Yeah, I do. What are you gonna do to 'em, sis?"

"I see you," Melanie taunts. "I see you. Come out, come out. You can't hide. All grown-ups sure think they're smarter than us kids. Think they can all team up on little ones. Well, don't forget, if your friends make themselves known to my friends, hidden or not, they fall under their spell. Cause this be my hallowed ground. I read your books. Come to hurt me, devils? *Well...my devils really are fixing to meet you.*"

Melanie sits down cross-legged in the middle of the living room. She tucks her head into her chest and curls her body into a muddy orb.

"Boy, you're gonna get it," says Winona, opening her eyes wide and shaking her head, watching from a window. She brushes back her hair, wiping drops of blood from her face.

Keep your book by your side, Liam. She can't strike you down if you hold on to your book.

"You sure about that?" Melanie asks, snickering, her head still buried in her chest. "Think the book protects him? This be my hallowed ground, ain't it? Why not show yourselves, sinners. Stop all your hiding. You're in his mind? Show yourselves to him. I reckon you're the ones who really want this fight with me now."

The house shakes as if there's an earthquake. Then thunder rumbles and lightning strikes outside, filling the room with bright light.

As the flash of lightning disappears, all the scarlet robes of the Abaddon Order appear in the flickering flames of the fireplace, surrounding me in the living room. It's as if they've been in the house all along. I recognize Silvia and Cline standing beside me. Kurt is walking around the others, ceremonially waving his sword. All the hoods of the order are drawn over their heads. But none of them seems to be aware that Melanie and I can see them.

Melanie sees them. She's looking right at them.

I hear whispering.

"I see you," Melanie says with a laugh. "Nasty, nasty sinners. Do you see 'em, Winnie?"

"*Sure do, sis!*" cries Winona, by the window, excitedly.

"What are you going to do to all of them, huh? What'cha gonna do?"

"Well, I just don't know. I don't know. I sort of think I should hurt 'em. That's what they want to do to us." She shrugs. "They come uninvited to Ma and Pa's house. That's sure rude." Melanie turns to me and smiles. "That's what you came to do to me, isn't it, warlock? Which one do you want me to harm first, mister? Why not I let you decide? You brought 'em here. How 'bout the big man dancing around with his big sword falls first?"

Kurt collapses to the ground.

Everyone huddles around him. His sleeve appears wet with a darker red. He cut himself and he's bleeding!

"He stabbed himself!"

"With our ceremonial sword!"

"Liam," Silvia cries, on her knees, searching around the room. "Liam, wherever you are! Whatever's happening, you have to fight the beast back! Otherwise she's going to kill all of us!"

"Manifesta, Abaddon Maga," I cry, holding the book before me. *"Manifesta. Abaddon Maga. Penitus. Penitus. Penitus. Show this girl what she abhors. Show her the witch she's become!"*

My friends disappear.

Melanie whirls around at me. She hisses. Then she jumps up, rushes to me, lifts her hand, and swats my book right out of my hands. *Broomstick* falls to the carpet.

Then she looks down at the book and gestures with her right hand toward the wall at the other side of the room. The book rises by itself into the air and is hurled across the room.

"I am witch!" she shouts at me. *"Me! I am! I am the Samhain Witch made by your own hands, you fool! I am the witch birthed forth upon this world that comes now every Samhain, every new year, to bring sinners to that which is*

vernal. Fire and destruction. Belial. Satan. That's what you wanted and that's what you get! Have you forgotten the last time you came to this house and cursed me? What do you think you're telling me now, in that fancy language of yours, that I don't already know? *Fear me!*" Her voice turns monstrous. "Hide behind your masks and feel afraid! For the Samhain Witch comes. And when she comes, she surely will come after you. And then she will burn all of you!"

"Kill him," Winona says, laughing outside the window. "Just kill him, sister. Kill him now."

Melanie bends forward. Her legs lengthen, her torso expands, and her arms flail out. The limbs lengthening reminds me of spider legs. Her torso is now large, with her clothes torn, and her whole body coated with filth and mud. Then her child's face lengthens to older features, like those of an adult, but still covered in mud.

She is now nearly my height. She's lengthened into some hideous adult version of herself. This is the vision of the older monster I remember from the restaurant. And with Melanie retaining those pearly-white eyes, she's just as hideous. No, more so.

"Kill him," Winona says, still laughing. "Just kill 'em now, and get this all over with."

"Get out of my house!" Melanie screams at me.

An invisible force lifts my body into the air. I find myself hovering for a moment, like Agnes once did.

Then my body is hurled across the room toward the open window. I'm violently smashed against the window, over and over, until my body finally breaks through.

When I hit the ground on my side, I catch Winona running back inside the house, staring over her shoulder at me. But as she rushes in, that now-adultlike hideous muddy creature follows. I'm on the brick porch. The only thing that stopped me from being hurled down the wild grassy hill below was an old rusty metal table. I look up and the sun has emerged from the clouds and is shining now. A black sun.

"Your friends left you," the muddy lady says with a shrug. Her voice has altered, sounding adult now. "Your life is forfeit. And now you will be destroyed. But before you pass on into the Summerland, I want you to know that this girl, Melanie, that you and your friends ruined, never once harmed you; nor your wife; nor all your friends. The girl only attacked when she was attacked. She never hurt anyone. Until now. Now you dare come back to murder her? After all the things you did to her? What sort of a little man are you that comes to hurt a child?"

The woman stares down at me with those hellish pearly-white eyes. Her adult body is now disgustingly vivid on the patio, lit by the black eclipsed sun above.

"Bear witness to the blessed gods that move the energies upon my sacred throne. *Keter* to *Thaumiel.* Crown to root. It is with sadness that we take away your energy, for you complete me. Heralding the sacred season of Samhain, I shall reign supreme every new year. Bear witness to your creation. For the next moon, by your blessing, I come forth to bring well wishes to all upon Samhain. I, your Samhain Witch, empress of all that holds power upon this earth every new year, come to destroy my kind. That. Is. Halloween. Then, circling once more upon *Ouroboros.* The circle of life, vile serpent. Your spell is complete. Witness the maiden become the mother. The mother be the harlot. The mother ends the green man. I shall haunt you every year after Mabon until midnight on Samhain. All my power shall burn bright until midnight before the time of All Hallows' Eve. Before the clock strikes thirteen, I shall will you, your wife, and all your friends to suffer intense pain and darkness in the world in which you reside. All thanks to this evocation."

"Venite foras," I say, closing my eyes in concentration. *"Venite foras, liber. Venite magus."*

I will the book, with all my intent, to return to my hand.

There's a crash of glass.

Melanie turns.

My Book of Shadows, my grimoire, *Broomstick,* launches through the window, just as I did. Melanie and I watch as the book circles in midair over the trees, quickly flying around the large grassy backyard glade, and then lands beside me. Grabbing it, I rise on my knees. Then I hold my book aloft before this monster.

She steps back.

"You're outside your house," I say, standing up with a smile. "That's outside your hallowed ground. Doesn't that make you weak?"

The monster opens those all-white eyes wide.

"Leave my sister alone!" screams Winona inside the house. "No! Don't you hurt her!"

"No," says a stranger's voice. I recognize Cadence from my vision. *"No, Liam. No! Please. This is your last chance to change the past! Please. Please don't do this. Don't hurt my friend!"*

Finish her now! Do it while you hold the book. It's either her or your wife!

"Exterminandi!" I shout, holding my book aloft. I will everything to be destroyed. The whole damned house. I want all of it to break into pieces. I don't want to see this damned horror house ever again. *"Exterminandi! Et advnit ira tua et tempus mortuorum! Exterminandi!"*

The Earth shakes. It's such a terrible quake that I'm thrown to the ground. This lady of mud falls too.

Then pieces from the house start falling. Rocks and stones, and tiles from the roof, tumble and crack. The entire house shifts to one side, as if shaking in an earthquake—so great a tremor that the walls from the first floor buckle.

Then the structure is violently thrown in the other direction.

The second floor falls onto the first floor, and this cascades into the walls crumbling. Fortunately for me, the home falls in the opposite direction. But the subsequent white clouds of dust and smoke are terrible, forcing me to cough and choke.

I scramble to my feet, rushing farther back down the grassy hillside toward the large forest glade, trying to run to safety from the falling structure.

As smoke clears, I see only rubble. But my ears are ringing.

I cough, wiping all the white dust from my face.

Melanie has shrunk back down to a little girl again, no longer covered with mud. Now her face and clothes are covered in white-gray chalk. The little girl turns back, gazing at me for a moment in utter confusion. Her whole face is covered in white, like a clown's face. But the whiteness of her eyes has left her. She turns back to the rubble and stumbles, trying to rise.

There's another crash. The final standing wall on the other side of the house collapses.

More stones fall near Melanie, forcing the little girl to step back. Then the girl wanders around the ruins. I don't understand why. She's climbing over stones, moving wood and drywall, looking under the cracks of the rocks and gravel.

"Winnie?" Melanie asks. It's Melanie's girl voice. "Winnie?" She's speaking quietly, as if in shock, but her voice seems loud in all the silence. "Winona? Winnie?"

There's nothing left of the place. Just a pile of rubble. "Winnie?"

Melanie freezes, staring down at something. Then she falls to her knees among the rubble. She screams. It's that same familiar scream I remember from during the spell in my backyard. It's not hideous, it's full of pain.

"Winnie! Winona! No, Winona! Winnie!"

She kneels, crying.

Slowly I stand up. I stumble toward the house—or what once was a house. Light brightens over the woods and surrounding grassy glade. Clouds disperse, but it's not the sun. The sun has been replaced by dim white moonlight. But that former black sun was so dark that the moonlight seems brighter.

I approach the little girl.

"She's dead," Melanie cries in her hands. "My sister is dead. My sister is dead," she repeats in tears. "Winona is dead. You killed her. You killed my sister."

Down among the rubble, I can just make out a small, pale, immobile hand. There's the sound of more stones falling. Melanie crawls over more stones and reaches for her sister's fingers. She touches the limp hand.

"You killed her," Melanie says, shaking her head. "My sister's dead. My God, you killed my sister."

16

NEVER AGAIN

I park behind a line of cars in the long driveway of my house. I recognize these cars parked behind our decorative red antique carriage. They're all Allie's friends from our coven. It's a bright, sunny day with clear skies. Something big is going down at the house this morning because it's Monday, not Friday, the day of our Sabbath. I have no idea what. I wouldn't know because I didn't call the hospital. I just got back from Alabama and didn't stop until I got home. My intention was to grab more of Allie's stuff and quickly head back to Hawthorne Hospital. But if all our friends are here, Alondra's either well or...something really horrible has happened. Whether wonderful or bad, honestly, I don't feel like I can take either news at the moment.

I stare forward. For a long time, I just sit under the morning sun staring out the windshield.

Then I cry.

I spent all night talking to the police. No matter how painful it was to stay by Melanie's house, I couldn't leave the place without making sure that someone helped the girl. Then...after I lied, saying that the house had collapsed before I arrived, the cops didn't arrest me. No one would believe the house fell down from *magic.* Cline was right about that.

Jesus... Melanie... I left her in her yard sobbing. Then I... apologized.

Why the fuck did I do that? Did I think that apologizing would help her? Well, apparently the shock of the house collapsing was enough to snap the girl out of her witch war with me. There was no more fighting.

Honestly, I don't have the energy to get out of the car.

"Liam!" cries a voice, hammering on my passenger window. It's blond-haired, smiley Rachel. And she's grimacing wider than ever.

I rub my eyes.

"Hey, Lee!" She is slapping the window. "She's better! She's better! Thank God! Allie's feeling better! Come in the house and see her, Lee. Come in and say hi!"

I roll down the window.

"Hey," Rachel says. Then she loses her smile and steps back. "What's the matter? Are you okay?"

Somehow, I get out of the car and walk with her to the front door. Then Rachel shouts that I'm here. That floods me with girls rushing up to greet me by the front door and embrace me. Their change in demeanor, becoming so smiley and happy, really couldn't be more jarring at the moment.

I feel like passing out.

But, following the crowds, not saying a word, I make it to the end of the hallway to the living room. Our sliding glass door is wide open, and I see a few of the girls outside. Some are walking by carrying white plastic chairs, heading to a stack of wood—our unlit bonfire—at the center of our back-yard. In the distance, I see Bill's in a black robe with Beth, heading back to the house. What are they preparing? It's not the Sabbath. Maybe because Allie's well, they're celebrating Samhain? But it's too early.

More of my friends rush outside to hug me.

Alondra's sitting in a white chair on the patio with five or six other witches sitting around her. Everyone is wearing black robes. She looks so weak and tired. There's a fluffy red blanket draped over her. But with all the hubbub, she's turned away from everyone, just staring at the woods. And she keeps closing her eyes.

"Look who the cat dragged in, High Priestess," teases Rachel.

"Oh, Lee," Allie says, turning with a smile. "Hi, Liam."

I rush over, put an arm around her, and kiss her cheek and forehead.

"Where were you, babe?" Alondra asks.

I shake my head and take a knee before her. Then I hold her hand, playing with her fingers.

"How are you feeling?" I ask.

"Better. Especially after seeing you. But...you—" She furrows her brow. "What's wrong? Have you been crying? What's the matter, babe?"

All the girls are standing over us, turning serious.

I shake my head.

"Hey, man!" hollers Bill, rushing from the house. "We were going to hold a ceremony to scry for you. Everybody was so worried."

I force myself up. Billy throws his arms around me.

"I was in Alabama."

Bill furrows his brow. So do Allie and the girls. But then, Alondra remembers her condition and leans back in her chair, putting her hand over her forehead. She closes her eyes.

"Can't talk about it now," I say to the coven.

Many just nod.

"You're feeling better, Alondra?"

"Yeah," she answers with a nod. But she still has her hand on her head. "I lost a lot of blood after the miscarriage. That's all it was, Liam."

Not a spell by Melanie to curse her.

Melanie, when changed to a woman, told me she didn't hurt Allie or Lucius. Maybe that was the truth? But now...I sure hurt Melanie.

It's too much. "I have to go. I'll be back soon." I reach down, squeeze Alondra's hand, and quickly head back inside the house.

And I'm off. Right through the sliding glass door, down the dim hall, and out through the front door. I hear a few of the girls yell something, but I don't turn back to find out what.

"Lee!" shouts Bill. "Liam!"

I'm back at my car.

"Lee!"

I unlock the door. Then I turn. Bill's running after me.

"Liam, where the hell are you going?"

"I can't stay. I've gotta...go do something. But tell Alondra I'll be back soon. I'm so happy she's better."

"Dude, she needs you *right now*, man," Bill says, grabbing my arm. "You can't go now."

"Hey, back off, man!" I snap, throwing his arm back. Then I look at his black robe with disgust.

"What the fuck is the matter with you?"

"Nothing."

"Look...you can't leave."

"Stay with her. Take care of her. I'll be right back, Billy, okay?"

"No, it's not okay. I was with her all night. And all she kept doing, even in sleep, was asking about you. *You*. You need to be with her, not me. She needs her *husband*. The doctors said she's lost a ton of blood. She's still really sick and weak. She needs you. You can't go now. Where the hell did you go yesterday, anyway? You said Alabama? Did you go to that freak house again?"

"Leave me alone, all right? I have to go do something. I'll be right back afterward. Okay? Look...just give me a little time. Tell her and the girls I'll be back. Tell Alondra that I'm so happy she's better, but I just need some time...alone. Right now, okay?"

He squints his eyes. Then finally, he lifts up his hands. "Okay. Okay. Sure. Go. Just get back as soon as you can. Man, Alondra needs you so much right now."

17

———

BURN MAGICK BURN

I'M FUCKING LEAVING HAWTHORNE. I KEEP GOING OVER IT again and again in my head. I want out. Maybe...god willing, with Alondra. Maybe not. Christ, I think she'll never leave. But maybe she'd leave if it was Hawthorne or me? Nope, not even then. It's like when she came back the last time I was through with her, handing me all those empty promises. What was I thinking? She's a wicked witch. She might be willing to leave the craft for a month or two, but she'll head right back. It's who she is. She says I'm the love of her life? But the thing is, so is witchcraft. Alondra *is* Hawthorne. And she's a witch. But...

I'm not a warlock.

I can't live like this. I can't even conceive of the idea of *studying* right now. I couldn't give a fuck about school. I feel so fucked up right now.

I park by our library—or the bulldozed remnants of it. That reminds me of Melanie's demolished house and I feel sick. Our student library has been upended and destroyed. That was so dumb. You'd think, because school's starting now, they could have scheduled the library's remodeling a few months ago, during the summer. Well, the parking lot, though quite empty despite it being early in the semester, is still intact.

So, near a dusty fence before a small bulldozer, I park my car. But I'm not here for the library.

I grab my book, take a lighter from the glove compartment, and then slam my car door, and I tuck my Book of Shadows, *Broomstick*, under my arm. Then I make my way around the fence to what was once the back of the library and into the dense woods.

I meander down a dirt path between the trees. And, after a bit of a trek, I start making my way uphill. For a moment, despite feeling so miserable, I realize that this trail is the one I took when I first saw my wife's witchcraft. That time I was accosted by two nude witches under the influence of drugs. Both became my friends. I pass the most treacherous part, where the ground narrows and there's a sheer drop down the hillside to the university. I walk beyond this spot then climb up higher until I enter a very large grassy field.

Here on Hilltop Bluff, in an open field in the woods, overlooking the campus, Hawthorne Forest stretches for as far as the eye can see. Beautiful, if I could give a shit right now. But the place is perfect for my secret plan of burning *Broomstick*.

But really, when you think about it, does it have to be secret? So what if a student sees me burning a book? I hear students burn their textbooks after finals all the time.

I forgot lighter fluid. Still, being that it's fall, with all these red and yellow leaves lying about, there's enough dry kindling. So I pile autumn leaves atop branches. After I've impatiently waited too long, my mini-bonfire starts burning in the center of the grassy field.

I drop my book into the fire.

"Burn, motherfucker. Burn. Fuck you and fuck Hawthorne."

I spit at it. My spit acts like gasoline fanning the flames. Even now, I suppose, even though I hate magic more than ever, I find myself casting spells to destroy the book.

The fire grows into a large bonfire. And there in the center burns my Book of Shadows.

So I turn away and walk toward the ledge. I am facing that sheer drop before Hawthorne University. Looking down, I can just make out the ruins of our library and the campus. On a long rocky ledge I sit cross-legged, smelling the wonderful scent of fresh woodsy air mixing with grimoire-ash, elm, and oak.

My eyes tear up again.

"I will never cast magic again. Never. I'm so sorry, Melanie. I'm so sorry for everything."

After an hour or so—I don't know, don't have my watch—I force myself to stand. Then I walk back to the fire. The flames are shallower now but still burning.

But then my body shakes. My Book of Shadows lies in the flames whole and intact. The fire didn't burn a thing.

18

HOME

It isn't until sunset that I arrive back home. I suppose, though I didn't realize it at the time, I wanted to wander around long enough to afford just enough time for everyone to go away. It's not that I didn't want to see them. I love my friends. I just didn't want to speak to anyone right now. Well, the plan worked. Under a clear evening sky, I don't spot even one vehicle on our driveway except that antique red carriage.

By the entryway, Sheba startles me by jumping into my arms.

"Liam?" Alondra asks weakly. Her voice seems to be coming from the upstairs bedroom. "Liam, is that you?"

"Yeah, Allie. I'm here."

Entering the bedroom, I find she's not in bed. She's wearing her black nightgown, sitting on our lounge chair by the window. She is turned away, staring out at our backyard forest glade. It's dark with only a dim light emanating from the living room window downstairs.

"How are you feeling?" I walk over, lean down, and kiss her cheek. I sit on the bed across from her.

"Better," she mutters with a nod.

I look over her shoulder toward the forest glade again.

And then, weirdly, neither of us says a thing. It's quiet. I mean, real quiet. Nearly quiet enough to hear crickets through a closed window.

"Will you be leaving again tonight?" she finally asks.

"No."

She nods solemnly. Then she's back to staring outside at the stars and trees.

"I burned the book. I went up to Hilltop Bluff. I started a fire and threw the book on branches and leaves and lit the book on fire. It couldn't burn, Allie. Even in all the flames of a bonfire. The fucking thing just wouldn't burn. I... I—" I shake my head vehemently. "It just couldn't. So I left the book there. And then I wandered around campus for hours. Because I didn't want to talk anymore. That's all. That's what I was doing. If you want the book, it's up on Hilltop Bluff, probably still sitting on broken logs and burnt grass."

I feel tears well up again. But, damn it, I'm not going to cry anymore.

"I don't want any of this shit anymore. I'm sorry, I'm done with all of it. I don't want magic, you and our friends' witchcraft, witches in Hawthorne. I'm done with all of it. It's all just magic and I don't want to be anywhere near any of it ever again."

"Okay, Lee."

"I know this isn't the time to talk about it," I say, jumping up. "Forget what I'm saying. You're sick. You need rest."

"Don't worry about me. But can't you...can you tell me why you're so upset? Bill told me you went back to Alabama? Did you see the Grant family again? Did you go into Winona's house?"

I walk to our floor-to-ceiling window and stare at the

stunning view from her bedroom, just like she is doing. The woods are so beautiful here. Beautiful, like my wife.

But dark. Cold.

"Did you put this window here?"

"What?" she asks, looking up, amused. "That's random, Liam. Mom did before she died. Mom loved this view upstairs. So did Dad. So did all my ancestors, I think, when they built the house. Of course, they say Maverick, Escoba's son, built the house. Maverick took over the whole town—so goes the myth. But Abigail's family, my side, eventually got it all back. I told you, Dad and I used to hike all over the forest when I was little. Why do you ask?"

"It's beautiful. Like you."

If it were during the day, we would see that those leaves are turning red and yellow to herald autumn. Now they're shadowed under moonlight.

I feel her watching me as I pace. I suppose I'd watch too. I can't stop moving.

"But the dining room was Jane's idea," she says. "We realized we had to use my dining room as another meeting place for the group during inclement weather. Jane suggested we make it look open downstairs too. And we both loved this bedroom window. So I listened to my best friend and added that window downstairs."

"Never mind the house, Liam, what the hell happened? You went back to Winona's house in Geneva Forest? Why? And why are you so jumpy? What happened in Alabama? God, babe, why can't you keep still?"

"I don't know if I can tell you."

"Then don't."

And she leans back in her chair and puts her head in her hand. This is so Alondra. Acting carefree about things, but sneakily using her keen mind, which is always thinking of what to plan next.

"Did you hurt Melanie?"

"*Yes!*"

Her body jumps.

Then I find myself plopping down on the mattress, this time with head in hands.

"*Fuck! I mean, FUCK! Fuck, I don't want this. I don't want to think about any of it anymore.*"

"Oh, baby," she mutters quietly, putting an arm around me. "Baby. Tell me what happened."

I marvel she had the strength to get up from the chair and embrace me.

"Tell me," she says quietly, rubbing my back. "Please. Please tell me. Why did you burn our book? What happened in Alabama? Please tell me, so I can try to help you."

"You can't help me now...anyway, you're sick."

She runs her hand through my hair.

"I...I didn't just hurt her. I killed her sister, Allie."

She falls silent. So quiet that I hear only her shallow breathing by my side. What can anyone say to that?

"No, Liam," she whispers quietly, "no. You would never do that."

"*I did!*" I snap. "I killed Winona, Alondra! A kid! I fought Melanie alone with that stupid book of yours. I demolished her house. Me, a grown man, attacked two poor little girls. With our magic. My spells. My incantations. My witchcraft."

And then I start fucking bawling. I can't hold it back anymore. And, however weak she is, she holds me.

"*By my...hands!*"

"Shh," she whispers. "Shh, it's over. It's done. Forget it. It's okay."

"*It's not okay!*"

And then I'm back to jumping up and stupidly pacing, a bit faster now, by the window. Part of me wants to run. She wouldn't stop me. It's like when she suggested I run from the dining room. Running away from everything is exactly what I want to do. She was so right. But I'm not crying anymore. I'm feeling really pissed.

"Forget I said anything."

She nods slowly.

"But you're not going to forget it, are you?" I ask angrily. "You're scheming with that wicked head of yours about what spell to cast next? What ritual we can try on our next Sabbath to make everything still work out all right? Well, that's why I burned the fucking book, Allie. Because no spell is ever going to bring back that kid's life. And now, I swear to you, I tell you, whatever the hell happens, I'm never uttering another spell ever again. Never. Never, ever again!"

"Okay, Liam," she says quietly.

And then I find that we've oddly switched sides. I'm sitting in the lounge chair and she's in bed. Part of me feels sick and dizzy, almost as if I'm the one suffering from her illness now.

She lies back in bed. And that makes me feel awful. She probably feels sicker due to all my yelling. So I force myself up and help her scoot toward the pillow.

Then I sit beside her.

"Lee...if you can, please don't leave tonight."

"I'm not going anywhere."

I turn and take her hand. I squeeze it. And then I run my hand through her bangs. In the moonlight through the window, I see her eyes shut.

"Lee," she mutters. "Tell me one more thing, Lee. Just answer one more thing and that'll be all. Did the Abaddon Order accompany you to that house in Alabama?"

"No one came with me to the house."

She nods weakly.

"They were with me in spirit. They used the book like a black mirror."

She just turns on her side away from me. I massage her back.

"Execrated," she mutters. "You were execrated. They cursed you, just like they said they would. The Abaddon Order was responsible for killing Winona and destroying the house, not you. I'm sure, with your heart, that you don't have it in you to kill a little girl. And now look what the curse has done to us."

"No, I killed her."

"Using the book, yes. It was your spell. But by your own intention? No. I don't believe that, Liam. Cline and Kurt of the Abaddon Order wanted to kill that little girl. They wanted to avenge the death of their leader. So if they couldn't kill the witch, they killed her sister."

"No, Alondra. I wanted, with all my intent, to destroy the house. I manifested it with the magic from *Broomstick*. No, I killed Winona."

19

BLUEGRASS

After driving up a constant incline on the highway for what seemed like hours, traversing mountaintops, and then coming back down along a very mountainous interstate, I take the off-ramp off the freeway. This drive is absolutely wonderful. Being close to Halloween, all the fall leaf colors on the trees of Kentucky are in full bloom, steeped in red, yellow, and orange. Hawthorne's tall, thin trees are pleasant enough, but Kentucky is known for some of the best-looking autumns in the country. The sky has been a bit overcast, but that's beautiful too.

When I'm down in spirits, I like driving alone. And this drive has really helped take my mind off things...a little. Well, I've got music from the band The Cranberries blaring through my car speakers, and I'm sipping a Coke slushy I bought from a Burger King. What more can one ask for?

The Burger King was really unique. Aside from the location being really picturesque, located in the mountains in a valley of rocky peaks, I was struck by the workers' accents. They were as thick as Alondra's uncle's, but totally Appalachian.

Now the presence of beautiful trees is dropping off a little, being replaced by a deep green grassland that's just as beautiful. I glance at the large, unfolded road map lying on the passenger side of my car. Parville. The address of the small town should be coming up now. I already scouted it out as being only about a half hour from the interstate. But this single-lane road is slowing me down.

And now I'm falling behind semis and cars that are lining up behind a black carriage led by a horse. Yeah, I'm not kidding. When I finally pass the cart, I see a man with a long white beard under a dark-brimmed hat holding the reins. Amish? Probably.

Finally I see a sign on the road telling me Parville is coming up in a few miles.

And then, in no time, I'm here. I see a two-story apartment complex. It, and a nearby small body of water, are the only things breaking up hills of deep green and autumn trees for miles. I throw my car door open and snatch my black jacket from the back seat. Then I make my way into the apartment building through its glass doors.

I glance at the note in my pants pocket. I'm looking for unit 103. When I find it, I knock on the door. Then I knock again, putting my thumbs in the pockets of my coat, waiting. And I wait... And then I wait some more. God, what if I drove eight hours, from dawn to noon, for nothing?

Light shines over toy cars and clothes strewn about on the carpet at the entryway as the door opens. Inside it's a total pig sty, with paper, open boxes, and crumpled cans all over the floor. To my left, I see a small hallway with two doors. To my right is a family room with a door that appears to exit into the grass fields. There's a nice smell of cinnamon in the air.

"Hi," says a little girl in front of me.

She's wearing a long white T-shirt down to her knees.

She has long disheveled dark hair and a mischievous smile. Her sly grin makes me shudder, sickly reminding me of that little rat, Melanie. But this girl is at least five years younger.

"Madison, won't you go finish your cereal?" hollers a woman's voice in a distinctive Southern accent. "Come on now. I'll get the door, honey."

"Bye, bye," the kid says with a smile and shrug. Then she turns her back on me, leaving the door wide open.

And that's when I see her. A lanky woman with long blond hair, wearing a simple white T-shirt and jeans, stands at the entryway staring at me.

"Liam?"

"Madison," she mumbles, turning back toward the kitchen. "Hey Madison! Hey, what did I tell you about opening the door for strangers?" But then she whirls back at me with a smile. "I mean, some people aren't strangers. Just...don't do that without Mommy ever again!"

"Hi, Jane."

"Hi, Lee," she says, turning back. But then she furrows her brow. Her grin sours to a frown. "Oh, Lee. What's happened?" She walks over and gently puts her arms around me. "Come in."

I follow Jane into the kitchen, where Madison is doing precisely what her mom told her to do. The little girl is busy with her spoon—which looks huge in her tiny fingers—as the kiddo dips it into the cereal bowl. She brings corn flakes and milk into her mouth, spilling a bit on her shirt, paying no attention to us.

"She's grown," I say with a chuckle.

Jane smiles and shrugs. "She's a handful." Jane runs her hand over the kid's long hair. "But I love her to death."

"Love you too, Momma," Madison says, between crunches.

I walk over and sit beside the toddler at the small round

table. She just keeps dipping her spoon in the bowl, ignoring me. Jane sits across from me. But then she jumps up. "Oh, you want coffee? Tea? Juice? It's near noon, I suppose."

"I don't need anything."

"I didn't expect you."

"I should have called. If you're busy, I can come back another time."

"Are you kidding? I told you that you can come anytime. Did you fly in? Or are you and Allie on vacation? Is she with you?"

"I came alone."

I glance around the kitchen. A window reveals a gorgeous view of the green grassy field that spreads out for miles with scattered orange- and red-leafed trees. It's interrupted only by the small pond in the distance. There are Halloween decorations throughout the room. Cardboard cut-outs of pumpkins and of witches with warts on their noses riding broomsticks are strung along the walls. Unlit candles are all over the counters. And there's a large black plastic cauldron filled with candy against the wall near the window.

The kid keeps crunching her cereal. But when I turn to her, she's staring right at me.

"Hi," she says.

"You got plans for Halloween?" I ask, pointing at all the decorations.

"Madison and I will go trick or treating. That's easy around here." Jane chuckles. "You just knock on your neighbor's door."

Jane rummages through the cabinets and pulls out a mug.

"I'm surprised by all the decorations," I say. "I would have thought with everything that happened—"

But I quickly clam up. The little tyke is staring at me. I'm remembering that this girl's parents were killed and Jane was convinced their death was caused by witchcraft. How stupid can I be? Do I really want to bring all that up now?

"I'm still a witch," Jane replies. She pours boiling water from a kettle into a mug. "I'll always be a witch. Nothing's ever going to take that away. But I'm a green witch now. I dabble only in herbs. Just good and simple things. That's all."

"Aunt Jane's a witch," says Madison with a nod. And then the girl bursts into laughter.

Jane hands me a steamy white mug.

"Like this tea," Jane says. She sits down, sipping her own black cup. "I made you something to calm your nerves and with just a little pep. You don't look like you've been sleeping."

"I haven't," I say with a shrug. "I've been driving."

"I'm Madison," the girl says.

"I know you are," I say, turning back to her with a laugh. "I saw you two years ago with your mom. You were just—" I indicated "tiny" with my two fingers. "Now I see you're all grown up."

"Hi," Madison says with a nod.

"Madison's my whole life," Jane says. "At first..." She throws her long blond hair back. "We came to Kentucky over a fling, Lee. I wrote to you about him. Things started out really well, but Lance was a jerk. Now Madison and I will be here just until the end of the year." Jane smiles wide. She touches the girl's arm as Madison spoons more cereal. "We'll live here together in peace for a little while till I find a job in Louisville or something. Until Yule. Here we can love one another. I really like just living with Madison. That's all I need in my life now."

I nod.

"But you, Lee... You..."

But then she doesn't say anything. She sips more of her tea instead, shaking her head.

"You know who you left, Jane."

"Yes," she says, nodding slowly. "I warned you about Alondra. You want to tell me what happened?"

But then I look at Madison. Maddie's back to digging into her bowl, but there's really not much there except left-over milk. She manages to get drops of white all over her arm. Then she looks up at her aunt—or her mom now, I suppose. Aunt Jane snatches a paper napkin near the bowl and wipes her arm and face.

"Maybe we should talk alone?" she suggests.

"It's okay."

"Madison," Jane says. "You're done with breakfast. Why not go and play in your room, sweetheart?"

Madison falls from her chair. "Bye," she says to me with a wave. Then she stumbles back to the hallway. I turn back to the view. And then I fall silent again, just staring at the beautiful dark-green grassy fields.

There's a noise from upstairs. And music is playing loud enough to shake the walls a little. Then someone stomps their feet. Apartment living, I suppose. But it doesn't seem to bother Jane. She seems more intent on me.

Jane finally turns to the hallway when we hear Madison walking back over carrying a small raggedy doll in both her arms. The little girl extends the doll out to me with outstretched hands.

"Do you want to play with my doll?"

My whole body shakes.

"Madison, go to your room!" Jane yells. *"I said leave us alone right now!"*

The poor little girl freaks out and rushes back down the hallway, crying.

I put my head in my hands.

"I'm...sorry."

"God, what is it, Lee?" Jane reaches over and touches my arm. "Why are you shaking so much? What's happened?"

"I don't know if I can say." Then I actually chuckle. "Funny, I came all the way here just to see you, Jane, and talk to you about it, thinking you might help. I'm glad I did. But now... I don't want to talk about it. Hawthorne. Magic. God, Alondra. I don't know if I can tell you about any of it."

"That bad, huh?" she asks quietly. She forces a smile. "Drink some tea. It might help."

But that makes me push the drink away. "I swore never to cast magic. I shouldn't be *drinking* magic either."

"It's just herbs I've gathered." She frowns and gestures at all the decorations. "You looked surprised that I have witch decorations? I told you, I had to leave Alondra, but I'll never leave witchcraft. I love our craft as much as she does. It's Alondra that I had to stay away from. I practice white magic now. It's the left-sided black magic that I promised never to practice again, Lee."

"Well, I don't care what direction magic is. I don't want to ever practice magic again."

She nods and sips tea.

"Congratulations, by the way," she says. "I got the invite for your wedding. I couldn't come because, you know, the way things turned out between Alondra and—"

"Alondra understood."

"She turned evil, Lee. That's why I left."

"Well, now I'm evil too."

"You're not evil," she says with a chuckle. "You've always been good, ever since I first met you."

That does it. I put my head in my hands and start crying like a stupid baby.

"Oh, Liam," she whispers. "God, what's the matter?"

"I killed a kid." The words barely come from my mouth. I'm not even sure Jane understood my words. But she says gently, "Tell me."

I wipe my eyes with the back of my hand.

"It's a long story."

"You drove a long way."

"I cast a spell and made a house fall on a little girl. That's all. There's nothing more to it. A girl died by my hands, Jane. By my witchcraft. That's why...I vow to never practice magic again."

And then I point at my tea and push it even farther from me.

Jane's just smiling woefully.

In my periphery, I catch little Madison in the hallway. That little stinker isn't crying now, she's snooping. Jane notices too and quickly gestures for her to shoo.

"What a ride life is," Jane says with a sigh. "Things seem to always be difficult. Why not take a walk with me? It's warm enough outside. I'll tell you my misery, and you tell me yours. I didn't kill anybody, but I did manage to hurt Madison."

I get up. And then my legs follow her.

She leads me into the small family room, where there's a simple fireplace and couch—and, of course, a ton more toys and trash lying about. Then she grabs a beige jacket draped on the sofa. We exit through the only door leading outside. Of course the little tyke is trailing right behind us.

"Madison," Jane says, turning to the girl, "no, you stay inside and *do not* open the door for anyone. Do you under-stand? No one. Don't do that again. If someone knocks, don't answer. We'll be walking outside and you can see us from the window and even holler if you need us. Okay?"

"Okay, Momma," she says with a nod.

"I mean it. Keep the door closed this time if anyone

knocks. Lee and I are just going to take a walk. Keep the doors locked and stay indoors."

She nods again.

"She's an angel," I say, walking outside.

Jane closes the door behind us.

"She's a devil," Jane says, shaking her head and locking the door. "But I love her more than anything in the world, Liam."

"You sacrificed a lot to take care of her."

Jane is pensive and quiet for a moment. Then she says with a shrug, "It's the best thing I ever did in my life."

And then we walk quietly. Which I don't mind.

She takes me past the parking lot and one-lane street, and then across into the grassy fields. The sky is clearing and the air smells fresh and clean. Everything is green. I take that in again. It's like there is as much wild green grass out here as Hawthorne has trees. Kentucky's known as the blue-grass state, isn't it? Well, here I can see miles and miles of that dark-green grass. In the distance, I spot the mountain I traversed, on the highway, to get down here. But the ground around Jane's apartment is flat. Very flat, but so beautiful, made even better by the sparse red-leafed trees here and there in the vista.

"Does she even know you came to visit me?" Jane finally asks, leading me onto a dirt path.

I shake my head.

"What are you going to do about school?"

"Fuck school," I say, heaving another sigh. "I can't care anymore. I'm not even sure I'm going to go back. My best friend left Duke just to join Alondra's cult. Everyone I know in Hawthorne is deep into her cult. I thought...stupidly, I could somehow stay with Alondra while 'ex-ing' out her witch stuff."

Jane shakes her head.

"Well, I tried. Even Alondra tried with me, I think. And you know what the worst part of it is, Jane? I still love her. We both still love each other."

"Over the years, every friend of Allie's eventually joined her coven," Jane said. "It was an unspoken rule. The quietest peer pressure. I think she would have been slower with you, if you hadn't discovered she was a witch when you first met her on Hilltop Bluff. Hawthorne is a cult, just like you said it is, Lee. Yes. Alondra's cult. But she had her way of convincing people that it's just a bunch of friends meeting every Friday night around a campfire. I suppose all cult leaders do that. Those that didn't join—" She shrugs. "She abandoned. I was the first to ever actually be the one to leave her."

"Well, Alondra and I got married because she was pregnant, Jane. I mean...well, we didn't marry just because of the baby. But we lost the child after she was starting to show."

"Oh, God, Lee, that's horrible, I'm so sorry."

"I mean, it was a miscarriage," I say with a shrug. "Allie and I were so excited about having a kid. The loss made her really depressed. She didn't want to go outside for weeks. This is Alondra, Jane. Alondra, who, you know, lives to be out in the fresh air. All she wanted to do was stay indoors. It's been hard—harder, I think, ever since you left us."

"I had to leave, Liam."

I nod.

Then we follow a dirt path to the left—the path is now surrounded by tall green grass. It looks like we're heading to the pond.

"So what about you?" I ask. "How the heck did you hurt Madison, Jane? She seems like a really happy kid."

"I fell in love with a jerk. I met him at the airport in Atlanta. He was an airline steward recently turned pilot, but his family lived in Kentucky. He loved it here. And that love for the area spread to me. I love the openness of the fields, just like I loved our trees back home in Flintwood. You picked the best time of the year to visit, you know. You see how beautiful fall is.

"Well, eventually the creep proposed. He even got me a really nice gold ring with a diamond. We were engaged—planned to marry last month. He wanted to be close to his sister here, in the small town he grew up in, so I agreed to move into the apartment with Madison. But I never really felt like we belonged here. I was willing to weather it all to be with Lance and raise Madison here. The plan was that when he got further along with his job, we'd buy a house closer to the city. I just wanted to be with him, you see. Until I found out that he wasn't always traveling to other cities to make money with the airlines. He was traveling, of course, to see another woman."

"I'm sorry, Jane."

"Yeah, well," she says with a sigh, "that seems to be my luck. But when I say he was a jerk, that's only because he was a cheat. He still had a heart. He's letting me and Maddie stay until the rental agreement ends at the start of next year. Between you and me, I think he still thinks there's hope for us. But that's like Alondra. Once they become bad, people will always be bad. People change a little, maybe, but certain things are unforgivable. I won't ever forgive Allie for tricking me into that satanic ritual in Bentmont, Liam. That was it between us. Really, even if the accident had never happened, I was ready to leave after that."

"But why'd you say you hurt Madison? Sounds like you guys were the ones hurt."

"Madison is stuck in the middle of nowhere because her crazy mom likes to be impulsive over love. Lance isn't the first one to cheat on me, Lee. Before Parville, it was Birmingham. Before Birmingham, it was Hinesville. I mean, it's a pretty town, but there's nothing here for us. And now, Madison and I don't know where to go. I'll have to take her out of school, for the third time, and maybe move back closer to Hawthorne. I prefer Georgia. Maybe we'll go to Flintwood, near Hawthorne, again. I don't know."

"It doesn't sound like you hurt Madison. You followed love."

"Ha, no. I followed passion. And I dragged my niece with me. No, I've screwed things up really bad for us. Well…" She sighs. "Never mind me. How 'bout you? I don't believe you are so bad as to purposefully kill a child. Can you tell me what happened?"

"Kenosha cursed the girl to get at Alondra. Just like she cursed me. The whole family was cursed."

"That bitch! She cursed a little girl too?"

"She cursed the whole family and their home to try to stop Allie's black magic. That curse led to the little girl becoming this possessed demon witch. Then, a couple weeks after Allie's miscarriage, Alondra fell sick. I thought it was Melanie attacking her. So I hunted Melanie, took down her house with a spell, and accidentally killed her sister."

"Well, I don't believe you hurt this girl intentionally."

"*Murdered,*" I snap. "*Murdered,* Jane. Melanie's sister died because of me. Because of *Broomstick.* And now Melanie, the poor surviving sister, is probably more bonkers than ever. All because of witches: Kenosha, Alondra, Agnes—even Agnes—and now *me.* Our magic and witchcraft completely destroyed her and her family."

We stop. Because the dirt path ends near the pond. Suits me well because, coincidentally, I have nothing more to say. I mean, what more can I say?

To my right is a tall tree with those distinctive pretty bright red leaves. The grass has some yellow but is mostly a dark green. The contrast of autumn with this green grass is absolutely wonderful. There's a horse grazing behind a wood fence to our right. And far beyond that, I see some concrete structures that are part of a farm. But it's all grassy slopes, otherwise, for miles.

"Forget it," I say. "None of this matters anymore."

"It matters a ton," she says, shaking her head. "Because it seems to be killing you. I warned you Alondra would hurt you if you stayed with her. Are you sure you're the only one who cast the spell that hurt this child?"

"What do you mean?"

"Well, when bad things used to happen with Alondra's spells—particularly a powerful incantation—things weren't always by her intent. As bad as Alondra is, she—like you—doesn't murder children. When people got terribly hurt by our spells, it was usually from some other bad witchcraft mixing in with the casting. You're sure Kenosha, or some other witch, didn't cast more mischief again?"

"She wasn't there. But, yes, another group followed me. They aren't witches, they're these Satanists and weird magicians. They used a black mirror to help me fight the girl. They were channeling through me and the book."

"*See, Lee!*" she snaps. "Then they're the ones who killed this girl, not you."

I shake my head. "That's what Alondra suggested. But Jane, I genuinely wanted the house destroyed."

"Lee, you tell me Alondra turned you bad? Okay. That's not an easy thing to do to a guy like you, but if anyone could do it, she could. I can believe that. But now you're suggesting that she turned you into some kind of child *murderer?*" She shakes her head. "No. I'd never believe that."

"It was an accident, but it was by my hand. If I threw a knife in the air and it accidentally fell through the kid's chest, wouldn't that be my fault too?"

"Not if someone else aimed the knife. Alondra was

wrong looking for a particular group that caused her parents' death. I don't think it was ever a specific group. I think it was multiple people. There are a lot of evil people in this world, Lee. What is the name of the group you're talking about? Maybe I've heard of them."

"They named themselves Abaddon."

"They actually call themselves *Abaddon*?" Jane asks incredulously. "Are you kidding me? Oh, come on. And you don't believe that they manipulated you? It's obvious."

"I miss you, Jane," I say with a nod and chuckle. "You always know the right things to say. I think, despite your fight with Allie, Alondra misses you terribly too."

"God, I miss you guys so much. But I'm not wise. I just told you that I moved Maddie and myself to the middle of nowhere over a filthy cheat."

We laugh.

"What are you going to do?" she asks. "Sounds like you don't have problems only with Alondra, you've got another psycho witch cursing you again."

"It doesn't matter. I'm not practicing magic ever again. I even tried to burn *Broomstick*. It wouldn't burn. It popped right back up inside our house."

"Then what are you going to do about Alondra?"

"What do you mean?"

"Are you going to leave her?"

I gaze out at the pond. A bird is gliding over the water right near us. There's a cool breeze. I squint up at the cerulean-blue sky with only a few wisps of white clouds. Then I take it all in with a deep breath, inhaling the fresh air.

Why did I drive all the way here? It wasn't for this blue-grass or fall colors. Am I hating Hawthorne and Alondra that much that I ran from her? Is Jane right?

Am I leaving her?

"I love her."

Jane nods.

"No, really, I do. And—" I shrug. "I can't stand her."

Jane laughs. Then she flashes a rueful grin and extends her arms for a hug.

"Sounds familiar," she says in my ear, hugging me and patting my back. "I love and hate her too. Don't worry. Things will work out."

Jane takes a deep breath, seemingly taking in the view of the grassland and pond before us too.

Then I yawn. I try to suppress it, but I can't. I didn't sleep all night.

"Why not rest here today," she says. "I can tell Madison really likes you. Stay and get some rest back at my apartment. I'll cook up some mac 'n' cheese." She smiles smugly and wags a finger. "But don't be thinking I can cook. I work herbs and potions, but, like Allie, I don't cook. But you and I can reminisce more over Hawthorne before you go. I really miss you, Liam."

"Me too. You're a great friend, Jane."

20

HALLOWEEN

Colored lights strobe through gray mist around a large forest glade, forming rainbows over the surrounding trees. The color illuminates the leaves and branches over a wild grassy field. This large wild grassy field reminds me of my backyard, only four times larger. It's a thick fog, so thick that it's turned this early afternoon into dark night. The main source of light comes from strobes and rainbow lights through the windows of the largest and oldest building in Hawthorne, The Billington frat house. I can smell the moisture in the mist. With the thick fog, it feels like it could be ten o'clock at night. But that's perfect for the party's ambience. The place is packed. And it's only gonna get more crowded. The colors flash and strobe over people's bodies. Shadows move among the trees too. Those are students coming to this rager. Though technically the party starts at six, my friends and I knew students would start congregating even in the early hours of the morning. That's how big this party is in Hawthorne.

Music blares. It isn't bad, it's some grunge stuff that Alondra and I like—it's just way too loud.

To add to all this surreal weirdness, the students of Hawthorne U. are wearing costumes. Most are gothic—ghosts, vampires, witches—but others, like a nearby Raggedy Ann and Andy and a girl in a skirt, with overdone blush and pom poms, are just plain fun. It's Halloween.

I sip beer from my red cup.

The house behind me is your typical fraternity house. There are posters of ladies in bikinis and cans and paper left on the carpet. Cracks in the walls and discolored paint. But also, as this is the oldest house in Hawthorne, there's a bunch of hundred-year-old antique furniture everywhere. None of my friends belong to the fraternity. But everybody in Hawthorne is invited. I think the whole goddamn town is here. Alondra really pissed this fraternity off when she stole all these guests, to party at her house instead, last year.

Billy's talking up a storm beside me with an Asian girl dressed in a golden fairy outfit. They're facing each other, playing with each other's fingers. I think he met the girl in Dr. Kriegel's class a couple months ago. But of course Bill's so sloshed that he barely knows where the fuck he is. We would have been indoors, but every room is already packed shoulder to shoulder. I suppose we'll have to come in the morning next year—that is, if Allie doesn't feel well enough to steal the show again.

"See, Rache, it's warm enough here. Liam and Bill are outside."

That's Beth. She walks outside with Rachel and Holly. Rachel is dressed up in a costume right out of the movie "Clueless," wearing a bright yellow jacket. She's Cher from that movie. And Beth is wearing a dark plaid suit and a large white top hat, matching Cher's best friend, Dionne. These are the same costumes they wore last year at Alondra's party when Alondra dressed as Gwen Stefani. Bill's just got an eyepatch and a red bandana with a black button-down and slacks.

"Hey, Lee," says Rachel, touching my arm, "is Falconsong coming?"

"I doubt it," I remark, shaking my head.

Rachel frowns.

I turn and Bill is totally making out with the fairy now.

"White Dove is going to do a reading for all these kids, Lee," Beth says with a wink. "She was thinking of showing everyone our coven's special tarot cards. But she was hoping she could get help from Falconsong. You know Alondra's always been the tarot expert."

"If you girls can find a spot," I say with a shrug. "This party is totally raging."

"Last year's party at your house was cooler," Rachel says, gazing behind her at the house.

I turn to Bill. The couple is groping one another now.

"Why don't you two get a room?"

"But his lips are so rummy," the girl says with a chuckle.

"You must be drinking as much as he is then," I quip with a laugh.

"Hey, fuck off, man," Bill drawls. But he laughs.

"*Fight! Fight!*"

There's a crash of glass behind me. Then, to my left, a guy is thrown outside, toppling over two old wicker chairs and slamming right onto a glass table. Quickly, a group of costumed onlookers runs out and circles the two drunken fools who are fighting. The onlookers are as surreal as ever, a motley mix of couples in white sheets, a really tall burly guy in a gladiator outfit, and the Raggedy Ann and Andy. Some are taking pictures with handheld cameras. Can you blame them? With the costumes, it's actually a little funny.

The guy dressed as a fast food cook with a paper hat tackles Dracula and starts slugging him mercilessly in the face. That's when the fast food guy grabs Beth's ankle and takes her down too. Dracula takes a swing at Beth. Luckily, Beth ducks, but the punch aimed toward my good friend makes me leap into the fray.

"Liam, be careful!" cries Rachel. "Be careful! Just get her out of—"

I grab Dracula's limp arm—he's clearly very drunk 'cause it's wobbly—and hit him viciously across the face. But the fast food hamburger guy seems to think it's all fun and games and swipes his elbow right into my nose.

"Look, knock it off!" I shout.

"Just break it up, guys!" cries Beth, scrambling up from her knees. "Stop. Stop fighting, okay!"

Blood is dripping from my nose. Bill is staring at the scene like an idiot, holding his new girlfriend in his arms. Some of the other girls from our coven manage to pull Beth out of the fight.

I slug the fast food guy in the face, knocking the jerk out. Then the stupid crowd cheers. When I move to Dracula again, Dracula puts his hands up. Then he runs in a panic toward the woods.

My gang helps me up.

"Abaddon," says a little girl in the distance. She giggles. "Abaddon."

This girl's voice seems so weird. I'm surrounded by all these costumed revelers staring at her.

"Abaddon."

I brush blood from my nose. Maybe I was hit too hard in the head?

"Abaddon."

It's a little girl's voice. Everyone in the backyard's now turned in her direction. There must be like fifty people staring at the wild grass and searching the trees for her.

A little girl emerges from a bright white cloud between

the trees. Sunlight creates a halo over her white dress as she meanders slowly across the grass toward the house. It's Melanie!

"Abaddon," she mutters again, chuckling. "Abaddon."

The white dress is filthy and in tatters. But she's not as muddy as her usual disgusting self. The dress is filthy, but it looks more old and dusty than muddy. Her hands and face are a little smudged too.

"Abaddon," she says, nodding and gazing up at the crowd. "Abaddon."

More people gather, staring at her.

"Are you okay, sweetie?" asks a lady in a Greek goddess costume, kneeling down beside her. Melanie nods as the lady places a hand on her shoulder. Her hand doesn't go through the girl's arm. So...this isn't an illusion. The girl is actually here.

"Aha," Melanie says with a nod again. "I sure am. Is that Liam Johansen over there?" The girl points, with an outstretched arm, at me. "That Alondra's husband? I need to talk to Alondra's husband for a second. I sure came a long way to talk to my papa."

"Oh, is that your daddy, sweetie?"

"Aha," she says with a nod and smile. "Aha. Yep, it sure is."

I wipe my nose. It's still dripping blood.

"Can I go see him?" Melanie asks, looking up at the lady.

"Sure you can, sweetheart. Sure." She holds the girl's hand and walks to me. "We'll get you back to your daddy."

Two couples right next to me, one in white sheets and another in military garb, are staring at me. Actually, everyone's turned from the girl to me.

"Happy Halloween, everybody," Melanie says with a big grimace. "Happy Halloween."

Melanie is escorted right to me.

I start shaking. I can't control my body. Then she makes it worse by throwing her arms around my waist, hugging me tightly. She doesn't stink. She's just a little girl. It's then I realize that, being Alondra's not here, no one, not even members of my own coven, know who the hell this girl is.

"Happy Halloween, Daddy," says Melanie, still squeezing me tightly. "I'm back."

"*Aw,*" say a few of the girls. Many others laugh. "She's so cute."

"What are you doing here?" I snap.

"I'm the Samhain Witch, remember, Papa? Samhain is the wonderful and happy season of Halloween. You made that my Sabbat. Remember? Happy Halloween everybody. Happy Halloween!"

All the costumed onlookers just nod at her, wave, and smile.

"She's so adorable," one of them says.

"Is that dirt or a costume?" asks another.

For all they know, it could be an adorable kid in a costume. But I think it's the girl's guile. She wouldn't be so cute if she were her usual stinky, muddy, horrid self.

"I'm...sorry," I stumble. But my words don't come out sounding like an apology. It sounds guarded. And that's terrible because these past couple weeks, all I've wanted to do is apologize to her again. I feel so uptight. No...scared. I'm terrified of her. That's why my whole body is still shaking.

"Sorry about what, Dad?" she asks, looking up.

"I'm sorry about what happened...to your sister."

"Winona? Oh, she's right over there, silly."

And Melanie points to the trees. In the misty shadows, another girl in a matching white dress appears. But it's hard to make her out in the dark shadows. She stands by a tree trunk for a moment but then seems to be quickly pulled back behind the trees.

"Mama follows me too. Especially around Samhain, when I feel so happy and powerful. Everything is going to be just fine. You'll see. Remember, that's what the blue witch and your good ole friend, Jane, in Kentucky told you. Everything will just go absolutely fine."

Then the girl laughs. That makes the crowd laugh too.

"She's so cute," says a woman in a Supergirl outfit.

"Who's this girl, bub?" asks Bill, sipping some beer.

But then the girl's whole body starts shaking like I did.

"Oh, what's the matter, dear?" asks the blond woman in the goddess costume. "What's happening? Why, what's wrong?"

"I'm just...starting to get a little scared."

"Scared of what, child?"

"I need his help. They're scrying, Liam. Scrying. They can't be scrying and scrying all the time. You know how much I hate all them witches scrying and crying. They can't reach me, but...tonight is my night, and I've shielded myself for weeks up to Halloween. You see?" People around her nod. "But *tomorrow*. Now, tomorrow, nuh-uh, tomorrow Samhain's gonna be over. After midnight, I can't stop them from cursing me. Can you visit them, Daddy? You feel bad? Well...if you really want to apologize, go talk to them and tell them not to hurt me. Why, I'm just a poor little girl."

And then the girl wickedly grins. The lady in the gold costume just furrows her brow and looks back at me.

"What the hell is she talking about?" asks another bystander.

Everyone's staring at me now because they think I can translate her usual senseless rambling.

"Cursed Hawthorne," Melanie says, glowering at everyone. "They're planning to kill me. And it's all your fault. All of you. If you don't do something, witches, this poor little girl's gonna die. You know they hurt me before. Now, with or without you, they're planning to finish me off. So, you say sorry about Winona, Mr. Johansen? Aw…well, why don't you go back to their goddamn house in Carolina and tell them to stop fucking casting curses on me then, you fucking idiot?" People gasp. "I never, ever hurt 'em. I didn't. I never hurt your wicked sinner wife either. But I need you to fix this mess you made. Will you help me? Cast just a little spell with your book to protect little me one last time? You say you're sorry? Makes no bit of difference." And she shakes her head and scowls at me. "I don't need apologies. I need you to stop those grown-ups from cursing a poor little girl. If you wait till after midnight tonight, all my power will fade. Then they can finish me off. And then, my poor little snake, you'll have *my* blood on your hands too."

The little girl's grin widens more than ever.

"Is there something wrong with her head?" someone asks.

"Is she sick?"

"Will you go to Raleigh or not?" Melanie asks me.

"I'll talk to them."

"Go to the house tonight. *Tonight*. It has to be *tonight* before midnight. I see their plans for magic, and I'm in big trouble if you don't talk to them. You must stop them before midnight, or I will lose my protection and it'll be all over for me. Will you do it, Liam?"

I nod again.

"Blessed be," she says with a grimace, extending her arms. Then she laughs at everyone, seeming more joyous than ever. Many join in her laughter. "Blessed be everyone! Oh, blessed be to all of you! Oh, I love each and every single one of you at Hawthorne! I love all you precious students, parents, and witches. But now, you see, I have to go. See, I have to go back home and remove my costume for my family. They're all dead, you see. Every single one of my family is dead now. Pa. Winona. They all died. And it surely be no trick of mine. Nope. Sure isn't. Everyone in my family is dead, guys. But boy do I have a treat for you all tonight. *Boy do I!* Happy Halloween, kids! Happy Samhain, witches! *My, my, just trick or treat to everyone and everybody everywhere!*"

She stares up at everyone. Then her smile is replaced by a crinkled nose and a look of utter disgust.

"*Walpurgisnacht!*" she barks. "*Walpurgisnacht! Walpurgisnacht!*"

A fire erupts and envelops her entire body in flames. People jump back from her, but many can't escape the fire. Still, no one is singed. The flames were an illusion. Then Melanie vanishes as if she were never there.

I hear gasps. And a hundred costumed revelers stare at the spot where Melanie was. All that's left is a black charred spot on white concrete. This time, my hallucination of the girl was real, and, *this time*, all these witnesses in the Billington House backyard saw it.

The crowd disperses, unnaturally quiet after witnessing the freak. No one says a word.

But Rachel and the rest of our gang stare at me. All the while, the shouting and music behind me, where the horror show wasn't witnessed, continue.

The blood dripping from my nose snaps me out of it. That is followed by a sharp pain in my face.

I rush back into the house, holding my nose. Inside, the party's raging. It reminds me of Allie's party back home last year. The typical people are lying on the hallway floor making out. Trash is strewn on the carpet. And people keep rushing by us through the narrow hallway.

Bill and Rachel are trailing right behind me, dodging bodies too.

"That was Melanie, right?" Bill asks.

"Uh, yeah, Bill."

"What are you going to do?" Rachel asks.

"Go to Raleigh like she asked me to."

"What?" Bill asks, trying to grab my shoulder. He can't as two people try to budge around us in the busy corridor. "You crazy? We need to gather the whole group."

"Melanie was right," I say, shaking my head. "It's my fault she's in danger. Just like it's my fault that her sister died."

I have to shout just to be heard in all the mayhem.

And then we have to stop in our tracks in a line in the hallway. There are so many people in this hallway that everyone's stopped waiting for the crowd to thin out.

"The Abaddon Order helped me kill her sister," I say. "I hate Melanie, sure, but I don't want their circle to kill her."

"But how can you trust anything that freak just told you, Lee?" Rachel asks, as we start moving again. "And if they are endangering the girl, how do you know they won't go after you too?"

"Not sure I care anymore after what happened, Rache."

We pass the living room. This is the most famous part of the house. This is, according to the ghost legend, where Abigail stood by the window holding a candle by her chest. Typical of Hawthorne, and apropos to my current problems, it's not just a ghost story; it's some story about Escoba battling witches. Only in Hawthorne, right?

I'm out the front door. The party is so raging that three other people in silver robot costumes nearly hit us rushing through the front door.

There's a yellow glow from the sun near the college. The mist is clearing down there. But it's still darker than a normal afternoon.

"I don't trust Melanie, Rachel," I say to her, walking across the grass to a path under nearby trees. "But what she said, in madness, makes sense. Or—" I actually laugh.

"Some of it did. You saw her. She literally just materialized in the Billington yard. That wasn't a black mirror. Melanie was actually here in flesh and blood."

"Yeah, we saw it," Bill says. "Why would she need your protection if she can do that, Liam?"

"You heard her. She said her magic comes from Halloween. Well, tomorrow Halloween's over. I remember her saying something about magic empowering her during this time when I fought her at the house. Well, after midnight, she's right. Halloween will be over. All the nonsense in her raving actually makes sense. She's in danger and needs my help. That order still thinks she killed their leader. They still want her killed."

"Lee, if this girl can materialize like she was in a transporter out of Star Trek," Bill cries, "do you really think she needs you to talk to them?"

"Let's at least talk this over with Alondra, Liam," Rachel says with a nod.

"I can't have another girl's death on my hands," I say, shaking my head vehemently. "I can't live with that. I can barely live with this now. Melanie was never my enemy. That cult killed the girl—or helped me do it. Alondra and Jane were right about that. That order used me, guys. Now they're going to kill her."

"But let's talk it all over with Alondra," Bill says, grabbing my arm. "Come on, man, we need the circle. What are you going to do to that cult on their turf, anyway?"

"Bill's right, we need to stick with the coven," Rachel says.

I halt.

The lights still flicker, as people pass the windows of the Billington House, through the fog among the trees surrounding us. I'm near the dirt walkway that meanders down the hillside to the college. I put my head in my hand

and vehemently shake it again. Fortunately, unlike my inebriated friend, I barely went through a beer. I'm quite sober for an emergency this time. But my mood still makes me feel like shit.

"Rachel," I say, "Alondra could be anywhere. By the time you find her, it'll be way too late for me to make it to Raleigh before midnight. It's over a six-hour drive. I need to go talk to Silvia. That's all. She's my friend. I'm not planning on doing anything but talk to her about stopping any ritual they've planned."

"Just call then!" Bill insists.

"Sure. I'll try to reach them by phone. I'll also check the house before I go. But wish me a lot of luck. They never answer the phone and Alondra's rarely ever home at this hour."

"Oh, come on, man!" Bill snaps, running his fingers through his hair.

"Let's just try a ritual at the house," Rachel suggests. "We can cast a shield spell for Melanie instead."

"You heard what that freak-girl said," I object. "They're going to kill her after midnight if I don't stop them tonight. I have till midnight."

"Let me go with you then, man," Bill says, touching my arm.

"You're drunk!" I snap, opening my eyes wide, knocking his hand off me. "Stay here in Hawthorne. If you guys want to help me, look for Alondra. If you find her, tell her where I went. You guys want to cast a shield spell for Melanie, Rache? Fine. Please, by all means. But I'm going to talk to Silvia. Convince her and her friends that the girl didn't kill their leader, and stop them from attacking her. I just have to talk to them."

"Are you an idiot!" Bill cries. *"We need to do this together!"*

"He's stubborn like High Priestess," Rachel says with a

woeful grin. Then she sighs. "That's why they love each other so much."

"Those are my friends back home," I say. "They even tried to help Alondra when she was sick in the hospital. I just need to talk. If Melanie's right, I'll do everything I can to convince them not to attack her. That's all I'm doing. Then I'll come back to Hawthorne."

"Lee," Rachel says, shaking her head, "did you ever think that maybe all those trinkets they put on Alondra in the hospital were planted to curse you and kill Melanie?"

Yes. I have. Sure, I've thought of that.

But then my nose drips with blood. Fuck, I think that asshole might have actually broken my nose.

I jump in surprise. Rachel gathers me into her arms before I can say anything else. "I'm scared, Lee. Just take care of yourself. Please? Talk to them, fine, but if you have to leave, come right back. If you sense any trouble, get the hell out. Bill and I are going to go search all over campus for Falconsong."

"At least run back to the house and get *Broomstick*, man!" urges Bill.

"No. No more magic. Never again."

21

HELL HOUSE

ONCE AGAIN I FIND MYSELF ENTERING THAT FAMILIAR neighborhood with all those white homes, looking for the solitary dismal black one. Except this time, since it's late evening, I can only search for the raven-painted hell house by reflective streetlight. I see a group of shadowy figures with hoods over their heads walking the streets a block from my destination. They're wearing hoodies, not Druid cloaks, but in sweaters and baggy jeans they look like they're in for just as much trouble. The Abaddon Order's house was never in the best part of town. And...here's that damned address. 666. I spot the two-story pitch-black building amid the sea of white. I think my hatred of Doctor Campbell started after seeing his taste in decor.

After climbing up narrow red brick steps, I knock on their black door. And then I wonder what in the hell I'm doing here. Am I being controlled by another witch spell? Doesn't matter. Melanie, no matter how disgusting and vile a monster she is, is still just a kid.

A bald dark-skinned girl with shaved eyebrows, wearing a white T-shirt and baggy pants, opens the door. Darbie.

Behind her there is no smoke, like last time, but still the distinct smell of pot. I hear lots of murmuring, more than last time. Because it's late and still Halloween night. A younger girl, pale and wearing just a shirt, runs, laughing, while being chased by a guy in a Hawaiian shirt and white shorts. A few others run, laughing, with them across the room.

"I figured it wasn't a stray trick or treater this time," Darbie says. "You should have seen the treats Cline laid out. What are you doing here, Liam, at this hour?"

"Is Silvia here? I really just want to talk to her."

"Cline," Darbie howls, looking over her shoulder. "Hey, Cliney! We got a visitor." Darbie looks at me from head to toe with a smile. "A real familiar one."

"Give the stranger some candy and tell him to fuck off," says Cline from another room.

"He's not a stranger, Cline."

A guy freezes in his tracks behind Darbie. He's trying to light a pipe in his hand—a tall, lanky, pale guy, wearing only white shorts. I remember this guy from our last ceremony. I think his name is Clifton.

"Come in, brother," he says. "Come in. Ninety-three. Ninety-three. Ninety-three. What a blessing. But you should have called, dude."

The man reaches out a hand to shake.

"I did. I left a voicemail. You guys never answer the phone. I just really have to speak with Silvia tonight."

"Take him into the living room," Cline says from another room. "Silvia's upstairs showering. She'll be down in a moment."

And then Cliff walks me over to the same room where I met Lucius last year. I see those same scarlet walls, the same red as their robes, with sigils scratched on them. I sit down on a ratty couch. It's the same brown couch I sat on last time too. And then I see those same crystals, gems, bones, and cards. The room is lit by a handful of candles in front of the fireplace and on the tables. And there's their altar.

"Care for a joint, man?" Cliff asks, smoking his pipe.

"No thanks."

"Happy Halloween," he says. "Hey, did you bring your book?" Cliff flicks a lighter, trying to light his pipe again. "We'd love to perform magic with you tonight, man."

"No, the book's back home."

"Too bad. Well," Cliff says, slapping my shoulder, "Silvia'll be down soon." But then he stops before leaving the room, looking back. "Do you two got something going on, Liam?"

"We're just friends."

"Sure. Sure. Well, we've got lots of pizza left, brother. Do you like pepperoni?"

"No, I already ate. Thanks."

"Ninety-three, brother," he says and walks off. "Ninety-three. Ninety-three."

Then I feel uncomfortable. And after a couple more of the members of their Satan-worshipping cult greet me by the doorway, I'm pretty much left alone. Meanwhile, I hear laughing and shouting in adjacent rooms and thumping on the ceiling from people running around upstairs.

"Hey, Lee!" cries Silvia.

She's in a long thick white bathrobe and her long blond hair's still wet. I jump up and embrace her.

"So great to see you!" she says. "Happy Halloween. Or, is it still Halloween? Is it midnight yet?"

She shrugs and plops down on the other side of the couch. But then she reaches over and gently touches the bandage on my nose.

"Oh no. What happened to your nose?"

"Got into a fight. Look, I really have to talk to you right now."

"You came all this way just to talk? Must be pretty damn important."

"It is. I have to talk to you tonight. And you guys don't answer the phone."

"Yeah," she says with a chuckle. "Cline thinks we should just pull that stupid thing out from the wall already."

Speaking of Cline, I almost swear I see her in another room. A few others keep popping in near the door, snooping.

"Silvia," I say more quietly, "How much did you guys influence me that night when I went to Alabama? When I called last, I told you guys about the house coming down on the kids. Alondra thinks you guys helped me bring the house down. She thinks you were responsible for Winona's death."

"Wow, you were so down," she says with a frown. "But you cast the spell, not us. But...sure, if it'll make you feel better to think we did it, then I guess, sure. We did it, Liam. That's fine, a'ight?" She smiles. "We did it. Okay? Honestly, everyone here can't stand those two girls and we definitely wanted them hurt." Then she reaches up to my face again. "What happened to your nose? Ow. Who the hell did this to you..."

"Never mind," I say. Then I say, practically in a whisper, "Melanie appeared at the Halloween party at the Billington House. The girl's convinced you guys are going to attack her after midnight with ritual or ceremony. She says her power is weakened after Halloween. Are you guys planning on hurting her? I came to do anything I can to stop that. I don't want her hurt anymore after what happened to her sister."

Silvia glances over my shoulder toward the door. Then she leans real close. Too close. I lurch back, thinking she's reaching over to kiss my lips, but she snatches my wrist instead. Her hand is shaking. Then she whispers in my ear, "Get out. Get out now, Lee. Get out of the house while you still can." Then Silvia sits back and nods. She attempts a grin. I realize her smile is very fake. In fact, I think all her bubbliness this time, though usually characteristically *her*, is an act. She's scared. And she keeps glancing over my shoulder.

"It's so great to see you," Silvia says more loudly, followed by a strained chuckle.

I clam up. What the hell am I supposed to say now?

The group outside the door gathers. Silvia gestures with her eyes for me to turn. It seems everyone from the entire house is here now.

"Why don't we go take a walk outside, Lee?" Silvia asks. "You witches love the outdoors, don't you? Nature and all. You want to take a private walk with me tonight?"

"Sure. Yeah. Sure."

"But why would you want to go outside now, Nancy?" asks Cline, walking over. She has on her scarlet robe. "It's getting cold at this hour. And your brothers prefer you both stay. No, I think we should prepare the ritual right away, now that we are blessed with this witch's presence. Liam seems to have a particular affinity for the abomination. I see her follow his aura, just like we followed him. In fact, I feel her presence around him right now. I think now would be the perfect time to perform our ritual to finally take care of the beast. Now Liam can help us."

"He came just to say hi to me, Cline," Silvia snaps. "Okay? That's all. He's really messed up in the head after what happened. He doesn't want to do magic ever again. He told us that on the phone, remember? I'll throw something on, Liam—" She jumps up. "Grab my coat, and then we can have a walk together. Okay?"

"I knew something was going on between them," quips Cliff from the other room. Some of the others laugh.

"Sit the fuck down, Nancy," Cline demands with a fake grin. She sits on the lounge chair across from me, losing her smile. *"Now. Sit."*

"Leave him alone, Cline!" cries Silvia. *"Liam's my friend!"*

"Liam," Cline says, steepling her fingers, just like I recall her leader once doing in that chair. "Do you know what happened to Kurt after you visited that demon's house again?"

"No!" Silvia shouts, vehemently shaking her head. "Stop it. No. He had nothing to do with that, Cline. I told you guys, he's my friend."

"But Liam is my friend too. We're all friends in the doctor's house. Do you know what happened, Liam? Do you know what happened to Kurt when you visited Melanie?"

"No."

"Well..." Cline says with a smirk, looking down at her lap. Every member in the house is now standing by the door. And, far more menacing, they're all wearing their scarlet robes with hoods over their heads.

"Just let him go!" says Silvia. *"He didn't hurt our god!"*

"Is he brainwashing you?" Cline asks, looking back up. "Yes, I think yes, Cliff, you're right. After joining with their male warlock, Silvia is changing her allegiance. You care way too much for this witch. I think you're straying from the Qlippoth and becoming a moon worshipper, Nancy."

"You've always been a bitch, Cline. I should be so lucky as to be one of Alondra's witches. Now get the hell out of our way, guys." Silvia tugs my hand and hauls me up. But they're blocking the door. "Get the fuck out of our way! Let me and Lee just take a walk, a'ight!"

"No," Cline orders. "Sit them down, brothers."

"Cline!" shouts Silvia. *"Cline, stop it!"*

The group comes closer. Someone grabs for my arm.

"Hey, back off, man!" I shout, knocking his hand away.

"This will just take a moment, Liam," Cline says. "You came to talk, right? Well, have a seat and we can talk. You don't want to get into another fight tonight, do you? You sit back down too, Silvia."

"Fuck you!" Silvia yells. *"Leave my friend and me alone!"*

But we sit. We don't have a choice with all their red-robed clan standing over us.

"After following you astrally, in our little joint venture, to Alabama," Cline says. "Kurt was badly hurt, Liam. We had to take him to the hospital. Unlike your *witches,* like your wife, we're not averse to getting help from modern medicine. Well, Kurt ended up in the ICU. He was bleeding. Very similar to your wife. See, the tiny little cunt that you keep trying to help not only murdered our god, her spell made our newest leader—"

"There's no evidence she killed Lumi!" objects Silvia.

"She was standing over his dead body in our backyard, stupid!"

"That doesn't mean she killed him."

"You were in the ritual when Kurt stabbed himself, Nancy!" cries Cline. "You saw it with your own eyes. So shut the fuck up while I talk to our guest! I warn you. Speak again and our group will muzzle you! It's quite clear where your allegiance lies now."

Silvia just puts her head in her hands and starts crying.

"Kurt used our ceremonial sword, Liam," Cline continues with a nod, "stabbing himself." Many of the robed cult members nod too. "He ended up bleeding out. And, well —" She gestures with her two hands extended. "Now he's dead."

"That has nothing to do with Liam!" shouts Silvia. *"Let him go now, Cline! Leave him alone!"*

"I'm not doing anything to him," Cline says with a chuckle. "Liam is the leader of the Hawthorne coven. I would just like magic to help finish off the little cunt. Is that so much to ask? Then Liam may go back to his forest in peace."

"No!" Silvia shouts. "No! Leave my friend alone! He doesn't want to cast magic anymore."

But she can't move with all of them towering over her. So she goes back to holding her head in her hands, crying.

"I'm not my coven's leader," I say, trying to dodge bodies to get up too. "We told you that as a ruse to make peace with your order."

"Then you're blinder than I thought," Cline says, getting up. "Your power stems from your grimoire. *Broomstick* is your coven's book. Lucius knew that. The power of your circle was stolen by you from Falconsong. Possessing Escoba Hawthorne's book, you are more Hawthorne's leader than Alondra. You wield more power. So we shall use your coven's power to fight the girl. We shall have ceremony tonight. The demon brought you here to deal with us. I saw her come to your college party. It's very likely that you're being controlled by her right now. I can't know for sure...but you are very suggestible. You were with us, after all. I'll know if she's controlling you after we start our ceremony.

"We shall use your connection with the little piece of shit to bring her into our home. And then we will finish her. She thinks you can help her survive? The kid just sent her executioner. You shall lure her in with your power. She trusts you, in a sick way, even though you killed her sister, brought down her house, and cursed her family. Tonight, we will cast a spell together to kill her."

"I won't," I say. "I swore to never cast a spell again."

"Oh, you will," Cline says with a shrug. "Because you don't have a choice. Your presence is the spell, fool. If you survive, then we'll let you go." The bitch laughs. "But, I'm afraid, since you didn't bring your book, we'll have to bleed you. Familiar? You witches love sacrifice. I will bleed you, just like your wife and just like my good friend Kurt were bled."

"God, leave him alone!" screams Silvia. She lunges at Cline, but three men grab her and throw her back on the couch.

"He's our bait, brothers," Cline says, looking at the others. "Bind him!"

"Let him go, you bitch!" cries Silvia. *"I hate you!"*

"And bind her too," Cline says with a sigh. "The idiot will untie him the minute she gets the chance."

"You fucking bitch!" Silvia says, lunging at her again, held back by the men standing over her. *"I hate you! I told Lumi. I've always hated you! You're such a horrible person. I'm through with this place, I tell you. Through! I'm done with all of you! I renounce my membership in this organization!"*

They laugh. I don't. Silvia's quite serious and it's horrible seeing the most wonderful, happy spirit I've ever known look so miserable.

"Brothers, muzzle her," Cline says.

They grab her, throw her on her side, and tie her hands behind her back. I try to pull them off her, but there are too many of them pushing me back. Then, when Silvia nearly breaks free, Androgyne takes out a long black wand. She slashes the stick in the air before her, and an invisible force makes Silvia tumble back down onto the couch. They cover her mouth with gray duct tape.

I'm surely next. The men in scarlet robes grab for me. And then I find myself in the second row of the night, slugging whatever my fists come into contact with as they keep attempting to lock my arms back. I contact a jaw, then another face, but there are too many of them.

They rope me from behind like Silvia and then duct tape my mouth shut too.

Then all the scarlet robes leave the room.

Silvia and I are left alone on the couch in their altar. She looks over at me frowning. I yank at the ropes, but my wrists are bound. Silvia shakes her head and starts to cry again.

22

HERMETICISM AND THE
FALCONHEAD

I ALMOST FEEL AS IF THE GROUP'S PREPARATION FOR THEIR ceremony is as ritualistic as their curse will be. All the lights are off. I mean, every light. Even candles on the floor have been doused out. And so, every time the door opens and a body enters, it looks more like a shadow than an actual person. It's almost as if they've not only gagged me, but blindfolded me. And every time someone comes inside, scratching something on the ground, arranging things, or even moving a chair, I only see their shadow. I can't help but think this is intended to fuck with my mind before the actual spell.

They led us upstairs into a large room, made larger by the absence of furniture. When the door was open before, I noticed sheets had been used to cover the curtains on the three windows so there's no light coming from outside. It'd be nighttime anyway—though brighter than this.

They've sat me on the hard, cold wood floor with my hands tied in front of me. The room is cold too. Silvia's tied to a chair at the other side of the room. I hear her occasional muffled whimper, but, like me, she can't say a thing through the tape over her mouth.

A woman in a Druid robe walks over and kneels. In the slight crack of light from the door, I recognize Cline's horrid face.

"This is man's blade," Cline whispers to me, crouching closer on her knees. She brushes something cold along my cheek. Again, Silvia cries something inaudible under her gag. "I use my athame to fill my chalice. Hail Lucifer."

And then she hums.

"Hail, Lucifer," says a group quietly outside the door.

"Hail, Lucifer," Cline whispers close to my ear. "Ninety-three, brothers."

"Ninety-three. Ninety-three."

I feel a sharp sting in my hand. Then another man enters, lighting up the room again. I see a silver chalice under me collecting drops of my blood. Then their whole order enters in red hooded robes. A man disrobes, letting his clothes fall to the ground. He wields a sword, like Kurt once did, which he thrusts in the air. He slices the blade, turning in all four cardinal directions. Then he moves toward me for a fifth, completing what appears to be the invocation of the pentagram. Then I hear him utter the names of the angels Gabriel and Michael.

The door is shut and everything becomes very dark again. I can just make out the shadows of all the members of the order standing over me.

Cline strikes a match. I squint from its brightness. Then she lights a single candle on the ground before me, and it floods the room with more light than before.

"Behold fire," Cline whispers with a nod.

"The fire element," the group echoes, standing over us.

"Behold my water," she says. She spits on the candle.

"The water element," they echo.

"Behold, earth. Observe as I lay my fingers on the ground."

"Earth. It grounds us."

"Behold my words."

"As said by our god, you speak using air," the group echoes. "But like water, the mind is the spirit that translates and communes with all. You have completed our circle, blessed Androgyne. Thirty-three points as revealed by Mars five, and the six stars above, as engraved upon both columns of the absolute. Three, six, nine. Ninety-three, brothers. Ninety-three."

"Ninety-three," Cline says with a nod. "Allow our pentagram to move the pyramid of union with blessed alchemy. Sulfur, mercury, and salt form the blessed triangle that transmutes fire into gold."

And then they hum.

Cline rises.

"Our ritual is prepared, warlock," Cline says.

Another robed woman kneels by Cline and places a bowl on the ground. She takes the silver chalice of my blood and drips it into the larger bowl.

"You will drink this," Cline says, gesturing to the bowl, now in both hands. "This is our potion mixed with your essence. Liam, I do this not only to get back at that little witch, but to protect us. Don't be stupid thinking that she sent you for her protection. She sent you here as her black mirror. We used your book as a black mirror to reach her before. Now she uses you, yourself, as a reflection to attack us. But I will use that same mirror, *you*, to summon her. When she appears, as she did at your party, we will kill her for the death of Kurt and Doctor Campbell. And this time, unlike at your house, you won't interfere with us."

She smiles, looking creepy in the light of the single flickering candle. Then she pours some of the contents of the larger bowl back into the silver chalice.

"Your blood is now mixed with our special tea. Mixed with your essence. Drinking from this chalice, you will instantly fall into trance. Then, upon trance, you shall reveal mud."

She yanks the tape off my mouth.

"The hell I will!"

"Don't be afraid," Cline says, chuckling. "This tea was a favorite of the doctor's. It produces a short trip of only a few minutes, far shorter and more powerful than henbane."

"I just want all this to stop," I say. "I came here to protect the kid, Cline. I don't want anyone else getting hurt."

"The abomination lies to you. You witnessed her body materializing at the party. Such power doesn't need your protection. That girl is the most powerful witch I've ever known. She brought you to use you, just as we used you, to scry and attack. And so we accept her bait. Only we do not intend to let her rage with her magic. We intend to use magic of our own to trap her in our house. Or, as you witches call it, our hallowed ground."

"Hail Satan," whispers the group standing over us.

"Hail Satan," she says with a nod. Then she points at the chalice.

"Now drink, Liam. When I have this chalice raised to your lips, consume it. You need only a small taste. I assume you haven't drunk this tea before, college student?" The bitch laughs. "Maybe you have. If you don't drink, our ritual will become more painful. I'll be forced to bleed you to death."

Silvia starts going crazy in her chair across the room.

"So begins our ceremony," Cline says, looking up to the others. Then she nods at two people, who help lift the bowl before me.

"Hail Satan," they all echo.

"Hail Satan," Cline whispers with a nod.

She cuts my other hand. Then she drips more blood into the chalice.

As she cuts me with her athame, I feel panicked. Dizzy. Breathing so heavily. I'm beginning to realize that I might not get out of here alive.

"When the drink comes to your lips," Cline says, "I suggest you drink it. Waste this tea and I will lay you down and cut you. Either way, we shall have our sacrifice tonight and finally do what you failed to do at your house."

Cline nods. Then the chalice, held by two others in red robes, is pushed against my lips.

But there's a knock on the door. No, more like a pounding. Not only is it very dark in the room, it's also very quiet. So this pounding seems extremely loud.

"Open the door!" shouts a voice downstairs. *That's Alondra's voice!*

"Fuck!" Cline snaps. She sticks tape back over my lips and jumps up. "Darbie, go downstairs and greet Liam's wife! Tell her that he and Silvia went out for a walk. Make up some directions to get her lost. And then lock the door behind her."

"But what if she doesn't leave, Priestess?"

"Is this a trap?" Cline asks, spinning around at Silvia. "Did you invite him, Nancy, knowing Falconsong would follow and attack our house!" Cline rushes over and tears the tape off Silvia's mouth.

"Fuck!" Silvia cries out in pain. *"You... Fuck, you fucking bitch! I hate you so much!"*

"Speak now, Nancy!" Cline yells. "You idiot! As usual, you're risking the lives of every one of us in the order. Did you and the Hawthorne coven bring these witches here tonight?" Then Cline screams, *"Did she come to bring him his book!"*

"Yeah!" Silvia says. "Yeah, I sure did, Cline. I planned this whole scheme, just like you love to do in that fucked-up head of yours, to screw all my friends over. Man, I thought you were all my friends. You claim you practice Thelema? Did good ole Crowley threaten to bleed people to death? To murder people? You think Lumi would approve of all this? Our god respected Liam. Now you want to bleed my friend in Aiwass's temple!"

"Open the door now!" Alondra shouts downstairs.

"What do I do?" asks Darbie. "What do I do?"

Cline turns around and glares with such wrath that it nearly makes Darbie trip over.

"Alondra is just a person!" shouts Cline. "Even if she's got the book, it's his power, not hers! Just open the fucking door! Tell her that he went for a walk, you idiot!"

Darbie nods and rushes out the door.

"I hate you!" shouts Silvia. *"I hate you!"*

I pull at the ropes. But unlike Silvia, who's in a chair, I'm sitting on the hard floor.

"You think killing Liam is going to stop that girl from hunting you!" Silvia shouts. Then she laughs. "That little child is coming for you, Cline. Don't you get it? The kid's gonna do the same thing she did to Lumi and Kurt to every one of you losers! The name Abaddon was almost a joke to the doctor. Lumi never worshipped the devil. He believed in both trees of life. He didn't just worship Lilith, like you, bitch. But you never got Lumi's punch line, did you? You call me stupid? Do you think the doctor would have tied Liam up to sacrifice him to kill a little kid! You think you're protecting us? You disgust me!"

"Shut up!" screams Cline again.

"You're one sick cookie, Cline," Silvia says, shaking her head and laughing.

But Cline pulls out her wand. Silvia lurches back, losing her grin.

"Don't hurt her!" warns one of the others standing near me.

"*Where is he!*" shouts Alondra downstairs. "What are you doing to Lee! Show me where Liam is now!"

"I told you—"

"*PROHIBE!*"

Alondra's shout is followed by the sound of a thud. I think that's Darbie's body hitting the ground.

"Falconsong's spellcasting," Cline says. "Terry, Cliff, Mona, rush downstairs. Lead her here to us. Get her into this room and I'll deal with her. Our room is prepared for the curse. We can add her energies to the temple."

"I hope she fucking kills you, Cline," Silvia says, laughing.

"What does it take to shut you up?"

"*Liam!*" cries Alondra. "*Lee!*"

"He's not here," says a voice. It sounds like the voice is coming from right outside the door.

"Don't lie to me," Alondra warns. "You freaks have him locked up somewhere? Show me where he is or I'll tear this house to the ground."

"This isn't your hallowed ground," says another stranger's voice.

"Darbie told you, Alondra," says Cliff. "He went out for a walk with Silvia. What the hell did you do to Darbie down there?"

"Exactly what I'm going to do to you if you don't fess up! Where is he!"

I feel another sharp burn. It's Cline. She's on her knees cutting my arm now!

"Leave him alone!" Silvia cries out.

"Tape her fucking mouth, I say!" cries Cline.

"CADAS!" Alondra shouts. I hear a tumbling sound. It sounds like someone's fallen down the stairs.

"Who are you?" shouts Alondra.

"Mona. I'm Mona. Don't hurt me, Falconsong. Please. No, don't."

"Just tell me where he is!"

"He's upstairs in the loft. Everyone in the house is upstairs performing a ritual in our temple."

Cline lifts my hand and lets more blood drip into the bowl.

"Adramelch," Cline whispers quietly over the chalice, closing her eyes. She runs a hand over the single candle. Then she whispers in my ear, *"Beleth. Marduk. Lucifer. Lucifer. Light my fire. Lucifer. Light my fire. As the black star rises, unveil shadows. Reveal filth and mud. Revelare. Revelare. Revelare. Bring me the child so that I may kill her."*

Then Cline brings the cold blade up to my neck.

"Liam," says Cline, "my day job is working in a hospital. I know all the arteries in your neck. So, I warn you this one last time. You'll die if you don't drink this potion. I'm out of time. I warn you. Take a sip of this tea or I will kill you right now."

She yanks off the tape. Then I feel them hold my head back.

"Alondra! Alondra!"

"Liam!"

"Open," Cline coaxes, pressing the blade closer to my throat. "Come on. Open your mouth now. It's your choice, warlock. Open your lips or else. The artery is close enough. A little closer and... Come on. That's it. Open..."

A bitter taste is on my lips. It tastes like burnt coffee or chocolate. Then, prying my lips open even more, the bitch manages to pour more than just a little taste...

23

TIME TO PLAY

"Isn't it interesting that in Celtic traditions, the May Queen is a triple goddess made up of three stages: the maiden, the mother, and the crone. Each stage represents a time in a lady's life. Her early life, where she is the maiden, fertile, exploring the world, like Persephone in her fields. The next is her middle stage, as a mother. And finally as an old woman. The three stages of life.

"So I'm proposing that these three stages are one and the same as the Eleusinian mysteries. Like Persephone, the woman roams her fields—she's fertile. She marries (though she was raped in the story because women were treated like complete trash back in ancient Greece). Finally Persephone returns to the earth. Reborn? Reincarnated? Perhaps that's the whole mystery in the ancient ritual?"

"Maybe the whole point was just to get high, Cadence?"

A bell tolls.

The ringing seems to reverberate and shake all the scarlet-robed figures still standing over me.

And then the bell tolls again.

"Aiwass," mutters Cline. She's sitting cross-legged beside

the bright candle before me. "Unveil shadow. Show yourself, Ekimmu."

"Time to come on out from where you're hiding now, Winnie!" cries Melanie, laughing. *"Come on out now, you hear?! Don't be afraid of these dumb, dumb sinners. It's time to play. Play, play, play!"*

The candle on the ground flickers. It goes in and out of focus. Then I see two. The wax cracks, forming lines into perfect pyramidal shapes within each column. The pyramids interlock into one Doric or papyrform-like column shape. Then the candles become solid. They lengthen until each one is as tall as a person, but still very thin, brightening into a brilliant white light shining all over the empty room. Surrounding the flames are triangles, squares, and diamonds. I realize these shapes make up the members of the Abaddon Order. And what was blurry and dark becomes clouded in a bright fluorescent blue light. And every man's or woman's robe seems to be made up of diamonds reflecting the cerulean and sapphire lights.

"Liam!"

The candles splinter into wood fibers. And then shapes spin around and around in a circle. There's a single red dot in the center of my vision, making me feel as if I'm rushing into a tunnel. But I realize the dot is the flame of the candle.

Bring her to me. Open. That's it. Open wide.

Melanie's laughing.

"My God, what have you done to him!" shouts Alondra. *"And Silvia? You bitch! You bound her too?"*

At the door, there's a black shade almost like an Ekimmu demon. But the cloak is solid onyx, and a hood is draped over her head. Alondra?

The door slams shut behind her. The slam is so loud, it shakes the entire room.

Then a girl laughs.

Cline comes in and out of focus, still kneeling before me. She stares at me with wide eyes.

"*Aiwass!*" Cline cries. "*Aiwass. Aiwass! I call upon you! Bring forth this filth so that I may sacrifice her upon your altar!*"

⁓

"*Ouroboros.*"

That's Melanie's voice, sounding strangely tranquil, as if in meditation.

"*Spiritus. Spiritus. Spiritus.* Devils shed your tails and come upon my hallowed ground. Hail the devils that come in peace. Show yourselves. For Samhain."

There's a flash of white light. Then, just as quickly, everything turns dark.

All is quiet.

I feel a gentle breeze blow over my face. And in the darkness, I realize I'm not alone. Surrounding me are the woods with tall black figures with shining white eyes standing behind branches and tree trunks. They wear the tattered dark cloaks of the Ekimmu. They stand everywhere, hiding among the shadows of the trees. I rub my eyes. This is my backyard, only it's nighttime now. The stars above are moving very fast, as if I'm passing through time. Every leaf and grass blade shines white, reflecting white moonlight. No...I watch as leaves rise, blossom, get coated in ice, return to dark green, then change to brown. I think I'm traveling through time, perceiving every season. And, for a moment, I fear that...if things don't slow down, I could become trapped in time.

Above me is the largest white moon I've ever seen.

I turn around and see my house. That familiar facade is comforting. Painted white, it seems brighter under the moonlight. My large bedroom window seems to reflect the moonlight, like a mirror.

Crickets chirp. Leaves stir.

I feel very afraid.

"Shed your tail and come forth, viper. *Spiritus. Spiritus. Spiritus. Burn the witch... Burn the witch... Burn the witch...*"

"I think I'm going to kill him, Cadence. I'm sorry. You and I won't need to go through all our pain if I just kill Liam and Alondra tonight. I think things will turn out just fine if I end everything now. The grown-ups have to go."

"But where will that lead you, Melanie?"

"Don't think it matters much anymore. Nope, I don't. Don't think anything matters anymore. No more Ma, no more Pa. No more Winnie. Why should anyone bother to listen to me? I'm just a kid. And it's all darkness and mud now."

"*Malkuth.* Mud. Without the ground there is no crown. *Keter.*"

"And without the moon there is no sun. *Qlippoth. Lilith* to *Thaumiel.* I read all your books of stars, Hawthorne Witch. You can't teach me much I don't already know. It won't change my mind."

"But you're my friend."

"Well, now I'm going to show them my friends."

"Please don't, Melanie."

"I be me, you be ewe. You wouldn't be you, you know, if it all never happened. Not sure we'd ever have met, dearest friend, if it hadn't turned out this way."

"I am you, Melanie. And I am you, Liam."

Wake up from this dream before it's too late, Liam. Hurry! Wake up. God, you just have to!

There, by the center of the wild grassy glade—before a very dim sapphire-flamed bonfire—sits a little girl, legs folded, in one of our black robes. Her face is covered in mud.

So is her tattered black robe. This woman stares forward with such intense focus. Melanie's not talking. She's humming.

"I'm sorry," I say. "I'm so sorry for what happened to your sister."

Melanie stops humming. She turns completely still. Then she looks up at me, furrowing her brow. Tears well in her eyes, but she doesn't look unhappy. In her bright pearly-white eyes, as white as the moonlight above, there's sheer venom and fury.

I turn, ready to run.

But she extends both hands toward the surrounding trees.

"Devil, you finally brought 'em to me, didn't you?" Melanie asks with a devilish grin. "All 'em sinners? Even that wicked sinner wife of yours? All according to plan. All according to plan. Now, by my altar, witness the birth of Hawthorne's greatest sacrifice. By you, Samael, and by you, Lilith, I reap mutual destruction. *Belial.*"

"I tried to stop them from hurting you."

"*Ghogiel,*" she says with a nod. "Did you happen to check the time, fool? It be the eleventh hour. *Belial.* Eleven thirty-six at night to be exact. The upside-down column. The Babylon scarlet harlot of the good book surely hasn't come yet to protect 'em sinners. And so, by blessed Hecate, upon *Qlippoth,* on this sacred Samhain night, I now gift to all witches that which is vernal."

"I'm sorry."

"The devils heard your atonement. Now you shall reap their punishment." Melanie grimaces and points her extended arm toward the trees. "*Ghogiel.* My friends now meet your friends. *Ouroboros.* Shed your tail. I enter their hallowed ground by your shadow for all of them to burn. All of you. *Burn!*"

"Burn. Burn. Burn!"

"No, please don't hurt them, Melanie!" cries Cadence in the wind.

"Well now, don't you worry!" Melanie shouts, looking up, bursting into laughter. *"I'm not gonna hurt 'em, Katie. I'm gonna burn 'em. I'm gonna burn 'em all real good! Each and every one of 'em. All's gonna get nice and crispy! All well done! Happy Walpurgis, witches! Well done! Well, well done!"*

"Liam! Run! Take Alondra and Silvia and get the hell out of the room now! Hurry! Wake up!"

"Walpurgisnacht! Walpurgisnacht! Walpurgisnacht!"

24

WELL DONE

Through white smoke I see Alondra, hooded in her black robe, crouched over me. Her face comes in and out of focus, pushing and pulling my shoulder, shaking me. And coughing. She keeps coughing like crazy, struggling to breathe.

"The door won't open!"

"She locked us in!"

"Trapped us!"

"I can't breathe!"

I cough. It's so hard to breathe.

There is a horrible smell of plastic and gasoline. And my chest hurts every time I take a deep breath. I see poor Silvia trying to free herself, still tied to the chair across the room. She's shouting something incomprehensible.

"Liam!" shouts Alondra. "Liam! Liam, wake up!"

My eyes flutter. They hurt to open. Then I cough like crazy.

For a moment, the darkness was pleasant—so much more pleasant than this hot, smoky room.

It's then that I remember I can't breathe.

A handful of people have pulled back the drapes from the two large windows in the room and now are hammering at the glass with their fists. Glass is shattering. But beyond the glass, they just hit boards. The three large windows are boarded up!

Everything's still lit by that single candle. But now a far brighter red hue of smoke emanates from the crack at the bottom of the door.

Alondra shakes me.

"Liam, wake up! *What did you creeps do to him!*"

"We're trapped!" says another voice. "The witch trapped us!"

"Alondra?" I mutter.

"Oh, Lee," she says. But then she tugs at me to stand. There's no way I'm doing that. I can barely sit. "Lee. Lee! Get up!"

I cough. I can't stop coughing.

"I think I've got the door."

"*No!*" screams Cline. She tugs at a scarlet-robed man working the door. *"Don't open the door! Just the windows! The fire is probably right outside—"*

Alondra covers me. I hear a rush of air. And then screaming. I see bodies burst into flames. Alondra's robe is on fire too and, somehow, I manage to take her back into my arms. She must have untied me.

I squint. The pitch-dark room is now bright with red and yellow flames. Another woman in scarlet rushes through the open doorway. She disappears into a wall of fire.

"We can't go through the door!" Cliff shouts. "The whole house is burning!"

"Break open the windows!" someone screams. "Come on,

the windows are the only way out! Break down the fucking windows now!"

They pound at the boards over the windows. But they can't break through.

This is it. I'm going to die here.

"Did Melanie somehow conjure those boards on the windows?" Alondra shouts.

"Lumi did!" Silvia cries back. "He was...keeping the temple dark for ceremony, Falconsong."

Poor Silvia. Is she still bound to the chair!? I can barely make her out through all the smoke.

Alondra sits on her knees facing the wall of fire. Then, holding *Broomstick* and raising her right palm toward the fire blazing in the doorway, she says, *"Prohibe. Prohibe. Extinguetur! Flamma succensionis extinguetur!"*

But nothing happens. All I hear is weeping, moaning, and coughing. And horrible screams.

"Just break the fucking boards!" someone shouts. *"Cast over the window, Falconsong!"*

Alondra crawls through thick smoke toward the windows. Struggling, she gets on a knee before one of the windows.

"Apertum!" Alondra shouts, holding my book aloft. *"Apertum!"*

But nothing happens... Except more screaming. And then... God, amid the yelling, I think I hear a little girl laughing.

Alondra moves close to me. There's still a taste of charred and burnt plastic on my tongue. Remnants of that fucking tea Cline drugged me with, or wood burning in the room? I don't know. I struggle to keep my eyes, which are tearing up, open in all the smoke.

"If we don't get out of here, Liam," Alondra says, panting.

"We're going to die. I need you...to cast a spell to break the boards on the windows with your book."

And she shoves the book into my hands.

"Silvia's tied to a chair," I say, shaking my head. "We have to help free her."

Jesus, bodies are burning by the door. I see bodies lying lifeless on the floor, by the door, covered in fire. I think Cline is one of them.

It's getting harder and harder to see. Before, I couldn't see because of the drug. Now the smoke is so thick that I see only a few feet in front of me. On one end of the room, toward the door, are blinding red flames. The other end is now a smoky black.

There's more hammering. I think people are throwing their bodies at the boarded windows.

"Lee," Alondra says. She runs a hand gently along my face. "Oh, Lee, Lee, baby." She shoves the book in my hands again. I keep pushing it away. "You left something of yours back home."

"No, Allie." I shake my head and close my eyes. "No way."

"Liam—" She puts an arm around me and whispers in my ear, "The book answers only to you now. It's your book. Melanie is stopping our magic with her magic. Your book is the only way out. She knew you wouldn't cast with it. It's the only way to get out of her trap."

"I killed a girl."

"*Use the book, Lee!*" yells Silvia. "*My God, you have to! Use the book now to help us, Lee! Please!*"

"If you don't cast magic," Alondra whispers, "we're going to die here. If I die with you...fine. But...but, you killed that girl for me. Because you love me, Liam. She died because you were protecting me. And now, you and I will die here if you don't do this one last spell."

I'm moving. I don't know how or why. Part of me isn't even sure if Alondra's dragging me. We have to crawl low to the ground because every time we rise we're met with too much smoke and we can't breathe. Every movement feels like someone put a hundred pounds on my back. It's so fucking hot. It's like we're crawling through coal and fire. But somehow I make it under the window. The slamming of bodies against the window has stopped. Because most are lying unconscious on the floor around us.

"Together," I say, weakly holding Allie's arm. Alondra nods. And then, with both hands together, somehow, we manage to rise to our knees. Holding my book, we recite: *"Apertum. Apertum, impero! Apertum! Apertum! Apertum!"*

The boards on the windows are blown asunder. But that's terrible because it fills the room with flames again! Fire explodes everywhere now. I think Alondra's and my bodies catch fire this time. But the outside brings air to breathe!

Someone crawls by us to the window and just falls out. Then comes another body.

Alondra helps me rise. We're right by the open windowsill, breathing in cold air. All we can do is fall.

Somehow we roll along the ground outside of the house.

We're free!

I hear sirens.

Alondra is by my side. She's so still, but her eyes are moving.

I turn.

The small black house is an inferno. And the flames are spreading to all the adjacent homes.

I see a transparent girl in our black robe weirdly standing on the sidewalk, staring up at the house. Melanie.

"Burn 'em witches," Melanie mutters solemnly, no longer in mirth, but in anger. "Burn 'em dry. Suck 'em tender, suck 'em dry. Suck and watch 'em all die. Suck 'em up lean, suck 'em up long. Suck 'em up forever in sinner song."

The little girl slowly nods.

"Verily, I say unto you, witch," Melanie says, cocking her head back to me. "Verily. Verily. All witches be free until next year. But watch out. For on Halloween, your Samhain Witch returns. Now by the loveliest dawn, I wish 'em witches a very happy All Saints' Day. Thy will be done, Liam. Well, well, well done. Now all these witches shall be very, very, very well done."

Then the little girl bursts into laughter as her little body bursts into flames. She disappears and her laughter is replaced by screaming from the house.

Alondra's eyes are shut. She's unconscious, lying beside me on the concrete. There's a horrible ache in my shoulder. I think I broke my fucking arm in the fall. But we're not on fire. And I can breathe.

I close my eyes to shut out a rush of red-and-blue flashing lights. And I hear more loud sirens.

But then I open my eyes thinking of...Silvia.

25

WANDERING

ALONDRA AND I ARE WANDERING QUIETLY TOGETHER ON A HIKE up a hillside between dead bushes and dense trees. We're in the mountains in a park called Maple Grove. It's about a two-hour drive up into the mountains from Mom's house in Raleigh. Out here, it's desolate. I remember camping by a tranquil stream farther down the valley with Billy and a bunch of high school friends years ago, so I suggested this spot to Allie. She loved the idea. Mainly because she wanted to get away from Mom, I think. Back home, they've been in shouting matches together. Honestly, I'm not sure how we're gonna survive staying at Mom's house this Christmas weekend.

Alondra can't hold my right hand because my right shoulder's in a sling. And her face is still bruised up. I feel like we're recovering from war. I suppose we are. A witch war.

This park is beautiful. Some of the trees are spiky and leafless, but most have red or yellow leaves still. We've walked past a number of waterfalls too. I saw remnants of snow along the highway on the way here, but the weather is warm enough today. Alondra's wearing an auburn sweater and jeans—she almost came in shorts. I'm in a hoodie and long shorts.

When I glance over, she's very serious. It's only when our eyes meet that there's a smile. She's so quiet. See, this is the solemn side of her that's the *real* her. It's so unlike the mask she wears with the other witches in her coven. Because she's still really depressed as hell over the miscarriage.

"How are you doing, Lee?" she asks.

I lead us uphill on a fork in the dirt path. I don't know why. We've never been here, but the way leads to a climb and, though I can't tell through all the trees and bushes, I'm hoping for a nicer view at the summit.

"I'm fine."

She just nods.

Then, only when a bird flutters close by and perches on a thorny bush, a pretty small bird with blue wings, does Allie take interest in something and smile. But when she approaches the bird, it darts off.

And we climb higher.

"I have to meet up with the girls next week, babe. We're going to celebrate Christmas our witchy way. You know, Yule. Of course you're invited. But you can stay inside if you want. It's not only important for us to meet for our holiday; it's vital to plan our defense. I have to find ways to protect us from now on."

"Protect us from what?"

"Melanie. You told me what she said. She told you she's going to haunt us every year now. I'll have to cast shield spells for our protection. That girl has enough bitterness to bring down all of Hawthorne next. I have to work on shield spells every year to protect us. I might even have to talk to the witch council and solicit that bitch Kenosha's help. It's all her fault, anyway."

"Thank God Silvia at least survived."

"Barely. Lee, this *Samhain Witch* managed to kill half of their order and nearly kill your good friend. And, not sure if you noticed, but every leader of their cult is dead—Cline, Kurt, and, of course, Lucius. That's not a coincidence." She slows as we're forced to climb some rocks on the trail. It's a bit of a hairy path with a sheer drop to my right. When we are finally in the clear, passing by an opening in the trees, she adds, "That little witch destroyed the Abaddon Order. She even schemed and brought you over from the Billington House party to kill you. She wanted both of us dead. I think Hawthorne is next. I can't let her attack the girls and—"

"Fine, Alondra. Fine. I don't want to talk about this."

"I'm just saying we'll have to meet and plan."

"It's your backyard."

That shuts her up. Because I said it more angrily than I intended.

Now we're meandering through a lot of trees, and it's becoming a little difficult to find the trail. The forest is thicker here, despite the lack of leaves. There's a wonderful fresh air smell mixed with the scent of earthy pine. These woods remind me a lot of Hawthorne.

"How's the arm?" she asks.

"It hurts like fucking hell. How's your leg?"

"My ankle's fine. I told you it was fine the day after the fall. But I also told you to take painkillers this morning, babe."

"No more drugs! No pain medicine or anything else."

"Sure, no drugs," she says, opening her eyes wide. Then she shrugs. "Sure thing."

Then she throws her long dark hair back, sighs, and stares off to the side as we continue our walk. Through some of the leaves, we can see a slope that heads down a valley. At the bottom of the valley is a view from the woods. She keeps staring, not, I think, because she cares for the view, but because she doesn't want to look at me.

I take a deep breath. Then I stop walking.

I put my left arm around her—the arm that isn't killing me. She leans into me. Then we ascend the dirt path as I squeeze her tightly and kiss her cheek.

"Do you like it here, Allie? Bill and I camped out here years ago. Of course, the fall leaves are down for winter. I was kind of hoping I could show you snow. But then it'd be too cold to hike. So it all works out, I suppose."

"I love it."

We climb a little more. And then voilà, I was right. We've made our way into a clearing and there's an amazing view of the valley of forests below. From here, we can make out miles and miles of trees. Behind us the mountains rise, covered white from snow. It reminds me a little of Hawthorne's Hilltop Bluff, only it's a far larger vista.

Alondra smiles. And I love that.

"It's beautiful," she says. "You were right. I love it." Then she snuggles closer to me. "Especially when you're here to warm me, Lee."

And we just gaze out at the vista holding each other.

"I'm sorry Mom and you are fighting," I say. "She's kinda ruining Christmas."

"She's more sensible than you."

"What?" I ask, lurching back. "What the hell is that supposed to mean?"

She turns and faces me. Gazing up into my eyes, she runs her palm through the hair on my cheek. I've grown a thick beard. It's temporary. But now that both Allie and I have asked for leave from school this semester and have become temporary hermits, I figured I could grow the facial hair out. Her forehead and cheek are still bruised. Noticing that makes me a little more upset.

She reaches up and gently kisses my lips.

"I love you, Alondra."

"I love you more than anything in this world, Liam." But then she loses her grin and looks down. "But your mom's right about me. It's been so hard for you because of *me*. Didn't you notice what happened when we walked through the door at her house? First she looked at your broken arm, then she glared at me. Because she hates me. Because she blames me for everything bad that's happened to us. And, hate to say it, she's right."

"Don't talk like that. No talking like this anymore. Remember?"

"On Halloween night, when the gang told me about Melanie's trap and that you were heading back alone to that snake lair, I had a lot of thinking to do on that drive. I realized that all of it, my pain, the baby, the hospital, endangering your very life, everything bad that's happened to you was because of me. I won't apologize for being a witch. Just like I could never apologize to Jane about that. I'll never do that. But, Liam, I will apologize for all the pain I've brought you. Especially for the baby. That I will do. For all of it, I'm sorry."

"We didn't lose the baby over witchcraft. Melanie made it clear—before trying to kill me—that she never attacked you. Our problems with the baby just happened, Allie."

"Witchcraft hurt you."

"I don't want to talk about it."

But that's terrible. Because it shuts her up again. She just nods solemnly, turning her back on me and gazing at the amazing view.

And isn't this the crux of our problems? The focus of everything bad in our relationship is witchcraft. I don't want to talk about it. But everything she is *is* witchcraft.

"At least Silvia's recovering."

"Silvia's suffering more pain than any of us now, Liam," Alondra says, shaking her head. "She was badly burned. Nothing has worked out well for us this year. Nothing. I… I just hope we can go back to a normal semester next year. And I hope you're planning on returning with me."

"Damn it, stop it!" I snap, turning to her. "Look, how can I get you out of this funk?"

"I'm fine, a'ight?!"

She's not fine. She's struggling with tears.

She walks a few paces along the hillside away from me. With her back turned, she just stares out at the valley below with her arms folded.

"I didn't want to be here!" she exclaims, shaking her head. "Liam, I wanted to be back home with my coven. Don't you get it? That's the other reason your mom and I are fighting. It's why *we're* fighting. I wanted to celebrate Yule with the girls. That's what I do every year back home. Liam, I'm a witch."

"I know."

"I know you know. *Shit!*"

"We'll just go back home then. I'll tell Mom that we can't stay for Christmas."

"Damn you, Liam! Stop being so fucking nice! We can't leave your mom on Christmas now. Your kindness hurts! It really hurts me!"

And then she falls apart. She just starts crying with her head in her hands. Allie never cries.

But I don't come over and put an arm around her to comfort her. I'm too upset myself.

"Allie, you have to get out of this funk."

"It's not you, Liam. I mean…you hurt Melanie for me."

"Stop fucking saying that!"

And she does. She stops crying. But she doesn't turn around.

"You keep saying over and over how all my pain was to protect you," I say with a sigh. "Did you ever think, Alondra, that I would have done the same for Silvia if she had been the one in the hospital?"

"No, Liam," she says, shaking her head with her back still to me. "No, no, I know you wouldn't have done what you did for me for her. Just like, after you swore to never cast magic again, you would never have cast magic in the burning house if it was just to save her. You did that for me too."

"I'm doing everything I can to make us happy."

She just looks up at the sky and nods. Then she wipes her eyes.

"How many times do we have to fight?"

"That's just it, babe," she says with a shrug. "It's not just me and your mom that are fighting. You know, that's the trouble with love. You can love someone so much, but still find them impossible to live with."

"So you find me impossible to live with?"

"Absolutely," she says, whirling around. But then she actually laughs in my face. She's smiling but wiping tears from her eyes. "Babe, I told you a moment ago that everything's my fault. Everything. There's nothing for us to fight about. But your mom hates me and there's really no sane reason that you shouldn't hate me now. Everything that you blame yourself for, Melanie, Winona, your possession when we met, I blame myself for. I take full responsibility for everything bad that happened to you."

"Damn you, Allie! That's not fair. I love you!"

"I know you do," she says with a nod, grinning.

"Then why the fuck are you smiling? Why is that funny?"

"Love is funny," she says with a shrug.

"Fuck you."

"See?"

"So, we're destined to fight forever?"

"Yeah, probably."

So this time, I'm the one who spins around and turns my back on her, staring out at the view. *I mean, fuck! Fuck! She's impossible!*

"Let's—" I run my hand through my hair. "Let's just invite the girls to my mom's house. We'll see if the coven can celebrate Christmas in Raleigh. We'll just get the whole gang up to North Carolina."

"There you go trying to fix the unfixable again. Your mom will never allow my friends to bring our cloaks, dance around a bonfire in her backyard, and build a labyrinth of candles by the neighborhood park."

"Then what the hell's the solution, Alondra?"

"There isn't one. I can't practice magic this Christmas because my husband insisted on being home with his mom. Of course, my coven would come here if I asked them to, but there's no way that my circle is going to be allowed to step through your mom's doorway in Druid clothes—though it would probably finally match your mom's expectations of her new daughter-in-law."

"Okay," I drawl, staring down the valley. "So...what do we do then, Allie?"

I jump as I feel her come from behind me and put her arm around me. She gently kisses my cheek and massages my back. Then she turns to me and her lips move to my lips.

"You can't fix this fucked-up world," she says quietly, between kisses. "Stop trying."

"But what do we do about *us*?"

"Well...as long as you're willing to hang with me, I'll love you to death." She gently kisses my lips. "So let's head back to your mommy's house. You can buy some earplugs at the corner 7-Eleven to help you sleep through the night with the shouting. And then, with our newfound family, we can open Christmas gifts and wish each other a merry fucking Christian Christmas."

"Sometimes I really hate you, Alondra."

"Hate you too, Lee. Oh—" she says, kissing my lips harder than ever. "I hate you so much sometimes that I want to tear you apart. Destroy you. Love you to pieces. Tear your shirt off. Yank off those shorts. And make mad love to you right here and now. So why don't we do that? Hmm? I haven't seen anyone pass by in the last hour. The ranger said this path is really secluded. Let's tear each other's clothes off and make mad love right here on the grass right now. It'll be like that time in Alabama at the cemetery. Seems you found the perfect private spot at this hilltop. Did you plan it, babe?"

"I don't plan things like you do," I say, reaching down and pecking her lips.

She laughs again.

"But I've also never made love to you with a broken arm."

"Yeah, well," she says, kissing me back. She carefully peels back my sweater from my arm. "It's warm enough, if we stay close in each other's arms. Nothing's going to ever get in the way of me loving you. Nothing. Nothing will ever do that."

26

CADENCE HAWTHORNE

OUROBOROS.

I say it aloud to myself. It's not a spell or incantation. It's an understanding. There's no one in my bedroom except a specter. A partly transparent man in a beige polo shirt, black pants, and slippers just staring through the floor-to-ceiling window at our backyard like a ghost. Liam Johansen. Looking over Liam's shoulder, I see a group of witches in black robes walking, holding hands, around and around a large bonfire in our backyard glade. My teacher, a very young version—nearly twenty years younger—is presiding over her coven. And all those other witches that have become familiar to me—and you—over the past few weeks, because of this cursed Book of Shadows, *Broomstick*—like Rachel, Beth, and Silvia—are down in the backyard glade too.

"*Ouroboros,*" I repeat out loud with a nod, closing my eyes.

"Now you got it, Cadence," Melanie's disembodied voice whispers. "*Ouroboros.*"

I shake my head and wipe tears from my eyes. I don't

want to cry, but finally understanding why Liam's been popping up from time to time in my bedroom for years makes me sad. And it's not just me that's crying. See, Liam's been crying. He's standing still, as if frozen in time, at the large window of my bedroom, gazing at the witches in ritual with those same tears welling up in his eyes.

Ouroboros.

I get it now. See, Liam never attended a ritual with Alondra again after they visited his mom on Christmas. The only time he ever cast magic again was to protect me, two decades later, in Alabama. And *Walpurgisnacht*? Well, Melanie, I understand that word too. Melanie wanted all of us to burn. Every single one of us. Even me.

"*Ouroboros*," I repeat aloud. "I understand now, Melanie. I went back to change the past. I so wanted to cast a spell to take away all your pain, and Liam's and Alondra's. I had the power, but it wasn't possible. How could I cast a spell to change the past when that past is what turned me into what I am? How can I cast a spell to end my ability to cast spells? Everything had to happen the way it did. And...if I had stopped your suffering, Melanie—the worst suffering of all of us—I wouldn't have ever come here to Hawthorne. And then I would never have met the love of my life. All your pain and my pain had to happen. *Ouroboros*. But...understanding it all doesn't make me happy. Do you understand, Melanie?"

"I sure do, Katie," she says morosely. "Sure do. I always understood. I'm pretty smart, you know. I learned a long time ago about that. It all kind of sucks, doesn't it?"

"All your pain and fury was for the balance," I say with a nod, still looking at Liam. "No, I'm sorry, Melanie. I'm so sorry for you. For Alondra, Liam, and all you guys' pain."

"Can't see why it took you so long to figure everything out. But, hey, are you and Maddie gonna come and visit me in Savannah in two weeks? It gets a bit lonely with just Bonnie around this time of year. Many of the girls have gone home to their families for the holidays. Not to mention, I think they're all crazy." Melanie cackles with laughter. "You know, when the snow starts clearing, Savannah is such a pretty town with all that Spanish moss you told me you love, Cadence. Are you going to come visit me up here with Maddie again? The view out my window gets really pretty. Can you come by?"

"I told you we would."

But then I break down and cry.

"Now, Katie. Now...now, now you stop that. Stop all your crying and crying. All you witches ever do is cry and cry and cry."

"I know. I know. I'm sorry. I just feel so bad for Liam and Alondra too. I... I need you to leave me alone right now, Melanie. I just need time alone. Go so I can be at peace. We'll come visit you with Madison and Aunt Jane in two weeks. Okay? I promise we will."

"Because you're my friend?"

"I'm your best friend."

"Well, Happy Yule, Cadence. And thanks for inviting me to your house for the party. You take care of that baby of yours, you hear? And don't be sad. Always remember that if you don't choose chocolate ice cream, you can always have strawberry. Or vanilla. But vanilla gets kind of boring."

She laughs. I nod and chuckle.

"Bye, Hawthorne Witch," she says. "Bye, bye."

"Bye, Samhain Witch. I love you."

And then I just stand there alone beside Liam's specter, staring at him. He's motionless, like a statue, just gazing out at the circle of black-robed witches dancing around the bonfire in our backyard. For so many years, I saw this vision. Never Alondra. I saw him even before I knew who Liam was.

He's kind of like that famous ghost in the Billington House, Abigail, that holds her candle by her chest while staring out at Hawthorne through a window. For the longest time, I thought I was seeing a ghost. You see, witches can see ghosts, and seeing them in Alondra's old house wouldn't be all that surprising to me. Only this figure never was a ghost. I found out later that Liam lives happily in New Jersey now and is very much alive. But I never understood why he appeared in Alondra's bedroom—now my bedroom— gazing through the window, down at the backyard glade, looking so sad. Until now.

God, Liam and Alondra loved each other so much that I think he left a part of his soul here.

"I didn't know, Alondra," I say out loud, looking up at the ceiling. "I always thought you had everything together. I just didn't know."

"Hey, Katie!" my hubby exclaims, bounding into the bedroom. Following him is yellow light from our outside hallway. "Everyone loved your Christmas party so much!"

But he steps back when I turn. He probably sees the stupid tears in my eyes. I wipe my eyes with the back of my hand and force a smile.

Liam disappears.

"What's the matter, babe?"

"Nothing," I say, forcing a smile and shaking my head. "Nothing. Forget it."

I plop down on the bed across from our window. He looks at the flickering candle on the nightstand and my book, *Broomstick*, open to the last page, behind me. And then, the love of my life plops down beside me.

"Cadence, are you reading that book again?" he asks solemnly, running his hand gently along my cheek.

"I'm the Hawthorne Witch," I say with a shrug. "Alondra's past is our past."

"What was in the book that spooked you this time? Enora?"

"Should I know something more about Enora?" I ask, opening my eyes wide. We laugh. Then I shake my head. "God, I thought we had it bad here in Hawthorne. I always thought that not understanding magic made life here so horrible, but it turns out that Alondra and Liam, knowing far more magic than we ever did, were so much more miserable than we could ever be. I've been reading their past. I had to know what changed and how, just how our whole mess began, and if, maybe, I could fix things for Melanie. I feel like... I mean, I would have appreciated if Alondra had told me, but you know how secretive she was. And Jane would never have opened up about all of it. So I took things into my own hands."

"Was it that bad?" he asks gently, wiping another tear from my eye.

"No." But then my voice breaks. "I mean, yes. Yes, it really was. It was horrible. They had it so hard. Shit...I don't want to cry. Especially after tonight. Tonight with our party and the gang opening Christmas gifts, everything was so magical. But, yes, Alondra's life in college was trying. And yes, it was terrifying. I just spoke with Melanie about it. She had the worst of it, of course."

"I thought she went home already?" he asks, looking around the room.

"I spoke with her spectrally. She understands. *Ouroboros*. It's all about *Ouroboros*: the circling tail of the serpent. I think even Alondra understood. See, Alondra always insisted on teaching me only good magic, not because she thought I would make a good witch without learning the bad, but because, I think, she knew she and Liam had already planted so much evil here in Hawthorne. You can't have good without bad. That's basic hermeticism. But that's not only occult magic, it's life. It's why Agnes and the witch council were so wrong, for so many years, about Melanie."

I take Mr. Handsome into my arms and squeeze him so tightly. Then I run my hand along the stubble of his cheek. He smiles as I lean over and kiss his soft lips.

"I'm so grateful for you and our friends, babe," I say. "For Jesus's blessings from above. Merry Christmas. I suppose everything worked out in the end, didn't it? See, the book also showed me that, had all that horrible stuff never happened to Alondra and to us in Hawthorne, we would never have been with each other."

"Please stop reading the book. Okay, Cadence?"

"Kiss me then," I say, shaking my head. "Kiss me...and love me. Yes, that's nice. Man, the party was so cool here, wasn't it? Even Kenosha loved it. We are so blessed with so many friends and family. Honestly, for so long I hated it in Hawthorne. I think, really, I only stayed for you."

"You're the Hawthorne Witch," he says with a shrug.

"I sure am," I say with a nod. Then I scowl, looking down. "And much nicer than the last one."

He gently lifts my chin. And then we press our lips together again, kissing for the longest time, just enjoying smooching, and enjoying our warmth and company together. It's wonderful, you know.

Merry Christmas everyone. Merry Christmas and Happy New Year! Halloween is the witches' New Year. Then six months later, halfway along the wheel of life every year, comes Beltane. So, I suppose, Happy Walpurgis, Melanie. Enjoy every season, guys. As our world spins round and round, we are blessed with every holiday celebrating life. That is *Ouroboros*.

"Happy Yule, Cadence," Melanie says. "But never Walpurgis again."

Fortunately my hubby doesn't hear her. He's too busy wonderfully smooching with me.

Merry Christmas, Melanie. Now shush, okay?

"Well, you're sure having a Merry Christmas right now in the arms of that fine man!"

"Okay," I say with a laugh. "Okay. Now scram."

Oops. I think my hubby heard that.

"Cadence, who are you talking to right now?"

"No one," I say with a laugh. "Nobody. Just kiss me, lover. Kiss me. And love me. I love you so much. Merry Christmas."

"Merry Christmas, Cadence. I love you."

THE END

WITCHY ADVENTURES ARE CONTINUED IN BROOMSTICK, BOOK 1, IN THE BESTSELLING HAWTHORNE UNIVERSITY WITCH SERIES ®

- BROOMSTICK
- WINDSTORM
- THE HAWTHORNE WITCH
- WITCH MIRROR
- RAVENS
- SHADOW CAST
- BELTANE FIRE short story prequel
- SAMHAIN WITCH short story (3.5)
- CANDY CRONE (6.5)

Don't forget, Alondra, Book of Shadow, & Walpurgis audiobooks narrated by Preston Geer and Alexa Elmy, are available everywhere where audiobooks are sold.

THE HAWTHORNE UNIVERSITY WITCH PREQUEL SERIES ®

- ALONDRA
- BOOK OF SHADOW
- WALPURGIS

EXCERPT FROM BOOK I

"CHAPTER 1 - HER AFFLICTION" IN BROOMSTICK, BOOK 1 OF THE HAWTHORNE UNIVERSITY WITCH SERIES BY A.L. HAWKE

I feel a chill in the air. But the sunlight flickers between fall leaves warming me as I walk across campus with my best friend, Madison. It will be winter soon, but for now, the last days of autumn in Georgia seem so peaceful. I glimpse at patches of blue through the canopy of trees. The sky is like … so perfect. I love fall, I really do.

But Maddie doesn't seem interested in Mother Nature. She's been acting like a witch since we got up, which is a bit odd because my BFF is one of the most energetic and cheery girls I know. I already asked her what's wrong, but she won't tell me.

We pass the dorms and climb the grassy hill at the center of campus. At the summit is the tallest building at Hawthorne University: our library. But we're not checking out books. A line of students snakes its way through a bunch of cute tables with burgundy umbrellas to the counter of our university coffee shop. I think the wait takes Maddie over the edge.

She finally starts spitting out the events of her evening. "I went out on a date with Patrick. You know, the guy in my film studies class." She told me about him before, emphasizing how tall and cute he is, but now she looks as if she bit into something sour. "I knew there was trouble the minute he picked me up in that filthy, dilapidated flatbed truck." (I'm not surprised. She's not a very good judge of character, you know). "We had this great tilapia chili dish and lime-green margaritas and everything was going fine until he reached under my skirt and touched my vagina." I look around me, biting my lip nervously. We're still standing in line, and she said the word *vagina* really loud. People are turning to look. Then Maddie tells me she hit him on the head. Patrick, acting like he was the victim, jumped up from their booth, ran, and left her the bill.

Anyway, Maddie's busy telling me this story about her date copping a feel—and saying the word *vagina* real loud—when, right before my eyes, she walks into the store and just grabs a drink off the counter. We haven't ordered anything yet. It looks like a latte, but I'm not sure. I'm not so sure she knows either. Then she grabs my arm and we make a hasty exit. Maddie is like a total kleptomaniac.

As we walk down a cement path paralleling the grassy hill, I stare at her and she flashes a really sweet grin, raising her cup as if in a toast. "Anyway, fuck him."

I'm thinking, *At least she was asked out on a date.*

She looks at the brew in her stolen cup, puzzled. Then she throws her long hair back and cocks her head toward me very earnestly, saying, "Alondra wants to meet you."

I'm still looking at her in shock.

"Why not?" Maddie asks. "It'll be fun."

But I'm not thinking about Alondra. I point at her cup.

"It's really good," she says with a chuckle. "I think it has soy. Want some? I don't usually order soy but...this isn't bad.

Look, Katie..." (People call me Katie a lot, even though my name is Cadence.) "Alondra says she wants to meet you outside of class. Just come with me to her house."

"I don't know," I say. "I don't like the look of her."

Now we're dodging bodies on the crowded lawn, heading to the main hall of the university. The main drag of Hawthorne is a white paved sidewalk surrounded by grass and trees, with brick buildings on both sides—and even more college bodies. The classroom buildings are spread out through the fields and under the tall trees. The leaves are so pretty in red and orange. Fall is my favorite time of year because I love the colors.

Hawthorne University is in Georgia. It's a really nice college, and I'm lucky to have been accepted here. So is Maddie. Everyone has a book tucked under their arm or is carrying a backpack. I have a pink backpack decorated with a unicorn. Maddie has always thought it's a little too cute, but I think it's whimsical. It even has purple swirls around the straps. Maddie's carrying a small book, but I'm pretty sure she won't read it. She's not the best student.

"You should go," Maddie says again, sipping her stolen drink. She runs her free hand through her hair, which is long and black like mine. I reach for my hair and realize I put it in a bun this morning, so I just pat the top of my head like an idiot. Then I think about Maddie's being a poor judge of character and think to myself, *No. No way am I going to Alondra's.*

"Why do you do that?" I point to her cup.

Then she drinks some more with a large grin. Again, she offers me some, but I don't have a chance to taste it because a nerdy-looking boy with glasses sprints between us, nearly knocking down her mysterious drink.

"Hey!" Maddie yells. "Watch where the fuck you're

going!" Then she turns back to me. "It's busy, Kate. We should have gone into town like I told you."

I shrug. "I thought we'd just spend the afternoon on the grass studying for midterms."

I must look hurt because Maddie giggles and runs her hand down my back. "Whatever. Whatever you want." Then she leans closer to me. "Just come with me tonight. Please. It'll be a lot of fun. Alondra's really nice. And I have a surprise."

"I don't know."

"Well…" Maddie walks off and stands under a really large tree. "You have to. For the surprise."

"Yeah? What?"

"Bryce will be there."

"So?"

"Whaddaya mean *so?*" she says. "You can't stop talking about him."

Of course Bryce will be there. He's my teaching assistant and is really hot. "You're just scared," I say. "Now you're trying to bribe me."

"I'm not scared, Cadence."

She plops down on the lawn, puts her book on her chest, and closes her eyes. I catch a glimpse of the book's cover. It features a burly man with rippling muscles and the title *Complete Me*. She's not studying.

"Just come," she says with her eyes closed. "I'll meet you back in our dorm at six to get ready."

"Are we eating there?"

"Yeah." Maddie laughs with her eyes still closed. "Alondra always has plenty to eat. Too much. She knows just how to fatten you up."

～

Dr. Alondra Johansen has a house in the middle of a thick forest, only a couple of miles from the university. It's rumored to have been built during the Civil War. I believe it. It's a white-columned two-story mansion with a large shaded patio and a beautiful paved walkway. It makes me think Scarlett O'Hara from *Gone with the Wind* is going to run down the steps, any minute, to greet us. Surrounding the walkway is a field of grass and tall trees, along with a garden full of white and red lilies. I like lilies. I don't like taking care of them, or any flowers for that matter, but I like looking at them. Especially in the wild. I like the outdoors. Always have.

A small wooden carriage, painted red, sits on a modern paved driveway alongside the property. Parked behind it is Dr. Johansen's dark gray Jaguar XJ. How does she own all this stuff? Some say she's the descendant of an old wealthy family. It can't be from her salary. She's my history professor.

There are others walking up the dirt walkway, mostly girls I recognize from class.

With all the grandeur of the mansion, I'm surprised to see Alondra herself greet us at the door. A long pitch-black cape is draped over a darker black silk shirt and slacks. She has long black hair like mine, hanging loosely in waves. This time I'm wearing my long hair down too. And like the times I've seen her in class, I'm struck by her eyes. Alondra has bright jade eyes, like jewels. Her skin is pale, much paler than mine, and for a moment I imagine that she's a vampire. It would certainly fit her affinity for the nineteenth century.

But her smile isn't sinister; it's sweet. She's always nice—too nice. She has a bright grin and seems thrilled to see me. "Cadence Hawthorne, come in." I'm a little surprised she remembers my name. "I'm so glad you came. Are you considering our project?"

"I'm thinking about it, Dr. Johansen."

Standing beside Alondra is her teaching assistant, the irresistibly yummy guy Maddie used to bribe me to come. Bryce's suit doesn't hide his muscular, athletic physique. He's looking down into my eyes too. But his eyes are blue—gorgeous blue. I'm reminded of the cover of that trashy romance novel my best friend was reading. The model was like a bulkier version of Bryce, but Bryce is the real deal—and incredibly hot.

Now I'm blushing.

"Cadence," Bryce says, taking my hand formally and tipping his head.

I'm cherry red.

Bryce turns to my friend. "Madison."

"Hi, Bryce," Maddie says. Then she looks at me and struggles not to laugh.

I look away.

The foyer is grand. Above me is this amazing chandelier. It's made of a hundred tiny crystals reflecting light. It's the most beautiful chandelier I've ever seen. I almost feel dizzy looking up at the twinkling crystals. But that doesn't do justice to the rest of the house. The hallway, including the wooden-railed stairway, is white, and marble columns frame the front door. Enormous windows extend from the ceilings to the travertine floor. The hallway leads to the kitchen, where everyone has gathered, their voices echoing through the house.

Dr. Johansen greets me as we linger just inside the doorway. "Please, call me Alondra." Oh yeah, my professor is still greeting me. Watching me. She's still looking at me with her mesmerizing green eyes. I completely forgot about her. I'm a little surprised she didn't say hello to Maddie. "You can reserve calling me by my title for when we're in class,

Cadence," she says with a nod. "But here, please relax. Call me Alondra."

Oh shit, do I not look relaxed?

My eyes fall on Maddie. My BFF bitch has the largest grimace I've seen in weeks.

"Come in, you two," Alondra says. "Make yourselves at home."

Make yourselves at home. And Alondra really seems to mean it. Bryce leads me to the kitchen, leaving the other two behind.

The kitchen is just as lovely as the entryway, with steel stoves, and marble—like *real* marble—countertops. It's all tidy and neat. About fifteen people are gathered in a small adjoining dining room, talking and laughing, their voices echoing through the large open spaces.

"You can help me with the trays," Bryce says with this amused smile. I catch his eyes straying along my shoulders and down my elegant black dress. It looks like he's thinking of something other than the trays.

What's on your mind, Bryce? ... Hope it's me.

"Sure," I say.

He collects glasses already full of champagne and places them on two trays. "How do you like our class?" he asks.

"It's good. I especially like ancient history and medieval times."

"Yeah," he says. "You know, I used to be interested in engineering, but that changed when I saw how much math I'd need to know." He chuckles. I ogle his lips and that to-die-for strong jawline as he laughs. I freeze for a second. I fight off a blush and hope he doesn't notice. "I suppose that's what fascinates me about witch trials," he says.

"It's all...fascinating," I say. "You really seem to be into Dr. Johansen's research."

He lifts the tray and places it in my hands. I'm extra careful, because my heart is beating so fast staring at those thick biceps, and the last thing I want to do is drop the tray. But Bryce is so cute.

TO BE CONTINUED IN BOOK I OF THE HAWTHORNE UNIVERSITY WITCH SERIES

ALSO BY A.L. HAWKE

PARANORMAL ROMANCE

- ALONDRA
- BOOK OF SHADOW
- WALPURGIS

- THE HAWTHORNE UNIVERSITY WITCH SERIES I-III
- THE HAWTHORNE UNIVERSITY WITCH SERIES 4-6
- THE HAWTHORNE UNIVERSITY WITCH HOLIDAY COLLECTION

- SHADES
- HAUNTING JOY
- PHANTOM MASQUERADE

- MY EVIL EYE
- THE GUARDIAN
- NECTAR OF AMBROSIA
- CORA

FANTASY: THE AZURE SERIES

- HARMONIA
- CORA: RISE OF THE FALLEN GODDESS
- AZURE BLUE
- CORAL RED
- PRINCESS SOJOURN

SCIENCE FICTION

- CANDY SAVANT SERIES

Books available at https://alhawke.com/books

PARTING WORDS

What did you think of *Walpurgis*? By placing a book review, you can inform others of your thoughts and help spread the word about my book.

Want more? Periodically I like to send news regarding current or new projects. If you'd like to be privy, I encourage you to sign up to my email newsletter. Your information will remain private and you can cancel any time.

Sign up at www.alhawke.com or scan the following QR code:

ABOUT THE AUTHOR

A.L. Hawke is the author of the bestselling Hawthorne University Witch series. The author lives in Southern California torching the midnight candle over lovers against a backdrop of machines, nymphs, magic, spice and mayhem. A.L. Hawke writes fantasy and romance spanning four thousand years, from pre-civilization to contemporary and beyond.

Visit A.L. Hawke at www.alhawke.com

Email: contact@alhawke.com

www.ingramcontent.com/pod-product-compliance
Lightning Source LLC
Chambersburg PA
CBHW032221190726
48289CB00007BA/2330